NO SMALL STORM

COAST TO COAST BRIDES 1

ANNE MATEER

ZB Zarephath Books

No Small Storm by Anne Mateer

Published by Zarephath Books
www.zarephathbooks.com

Scripture quotations are from the King James Version of the Bible.

This is a work of fiction. Names , characters, incidents, and dialogue are products
of the author's imagination and are not to be construed as real. Any resemblance
to events or persons, living or dead, is entirely coincidental.

Cover by Sarah Thompson Designs (photo by Tim Mossholder (Unsplash);
engraving via Creative Commons from *The History of the State of Rhode Island and
Providence Plantations* by Thomas Williams Bicknell, 1920.)

Ebook ISBN: 978-0-9992322-1-7
Print ISBN: 978-0-9992322-0-0

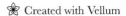 Created with Vellum

For my faithful readers—
Love for you compels me to keep telling stories

The floods have lifted up, O Lord,
The floods have lifted up their voice;
The floods lift up their waves.
The Lord on high is mightier than the noise of many waters,
Yea, than the mighty waves of the sea.
Psalm 93:3-4

CHAPTER 1

September 1815

REMEMBRANCE WILKINS—MEM to her friends and family—shivered, feeling to her bones the coolness of stone walls which never warmed. Eyes adjusting to the cellar's dimness, she lifted the candle lantern higher, wishing its small flame would throw out a bit of heat, as well as a larger circle of light.

There. In one of the perpetually shadowed corners, she spied a stack of bushel baskets within reach. Setting the lantern on the smooth dirt floor, she carefully unloaded the cloth bag at her hip. Apples. Twenty-two of them. Rhode Island greenings which would remain crisp and fresh in the cellar until the whole crop could be sold for transport beyond the port of Providence, Rhode Island. Or they were chosen for pressing into cider.

"But at this rate, I won't have a crop to sell until November!" Mem huffed the words under her breath, even though there wasn't a soul near enough to hear had she shouted. That was the glory of the farm—and the problem. Independence, yes. But often loneliness, too, if she were honest.

Her sister, Charity, often suggested hiring assistance, but Mem resisted. She needed the daily tasks to keep her occupied. And while a man in the fields would have his use, she had little desire for the help or company of any of that sex, now that her father had gone.

She lifted the lantern, the flickering candle inside barely skimming back the dark as she made her way back to the steps and into the sparkling day. In the flood of daylight, one quick breath extinguished the flame inside the lantern's iron frame. She set it on the ground as an errant curl tickled the side of her face. She hadn't time to stop and secure the wisp that had slipped loose of the pins. With squared shoulders, she stalked between rows of apple trees, all planted by her grandfather fifty years earlier, when Rhode Island was a colony, not a state. When this was British land, not American.

Near the back of the orchard, she spied the ladder still leaning against the trunk of a tree, its top lost in the profusion of leaves. Mem looked down at the yards of fabric covering her legs, wishing she could wear trousers, as her father had, instead of battling skirts and petticoats in order to secure an apple for her bag. But some things couldn't be wished away; they had to be endured. With the bag over her shoulder, she twisted her skirt and secured it between her knees. Then she set her foot on the first rung.

A rustling noise stopped her ascent. Not the gentle chorus of a sweep of breeze over hundreds of leaves. More like—

There it was again. A shimmy and a shake from somewhere above her head. Mem tipped her chin skyward, ready to flap her apron at a bold bird seeking a taste of fruit.

But the intruder she spied was larger than any bird.

Much larger.

"What are you—?"

A golden-haired boy of perhaps ten dropped from the

branches and landed crouched on the ground. Mem stared at him for a long moment, neither of them moving. Then he sprang to his feet and dashed away. Jumping from the ladder, Mem darted after him, trying to keep her feet from getting tangled in her hem. A cackle from behind brought her to a halt. When it sounded again, she whipped around to find another boy, similar in size to the first, squatting in the grass beneath the same tree, apple in hand.

"Stop!" Her shout carried across the orchard as she ran toward the newest intruder. He stood slowly, as if he needn't fear she'd catch him before he could scamper out of reach. Then he sank his teeth into the firm flesh of one of her apples. Juice dripped down his chin, onto his shirt. He opened his mouth to take another bite just as Mem grasped his arm. With a saucy grin, he threw off her grip and darted off in the direction of his accomplice.

Within moments, Mem stood alone on the road just beyond her apple trees, hands on her hips, chest heaving, lips mashed into a tight line. She hadn't recognized the two urchins, but she'd remember their faces, keep a lookout for them. Although she doubted she had any chance of discovery since they weren't already known to her. The population of Providence had grown greatly in the past few years. And now that the war with Britain had drawn to a close, there were so many new faces in and out of port. Mem grunted as she straightened the bag that had twisted in her haste, making sure the opening hung just in front of her hip. Then she returned to her orchard and started into the treetops again, tucking her skirt between her legs and climbing the ladder.

Two apples. That was likely all the boys had pilfered. She hoped. She leaned against the top of the ladder with a sigh and twisted a greening until it broke free from the branch. After gently dropping it into her bag, Mem's fingers found the next ripe apple and repeated the process. It wasn't as if she couldn't afford to lose two apples. Not with the bumper crop that had sprouted this year. A crop Papa would have crowed over.

Her eyes burned with sudden tears. Tears of grief. Tears of gratitude. She missed Papa's presence, his quiet faith and booming laughter—the loss too recent to be considered without pain. But to have him bequeath her the farm, allow her to remain at home and work the land she loved? Mem's heart swelled thinking of the words Mr. Benson had read the day after Charity and Mem watched Papa returned to the earth.

To my daughter Remembrance Wilkins, I bequeath the family farm and orchard, the land and its prosperity, for her lifetime use, after which it will be divided among any surviving children issued from either Remembrance or her sister, Charity Wilkins Hyer.

A position of independence was not always afforded an unmarried daughter. But Papa had understood. Mem had trusted him to provide for her, and he hadn't betrayed that trust. Unlike another man she'd had the misfortune to know.

The bag at her side grew bulky as her fingers worked by rote and her mind wandered. Then she eased back down the ladder, retrieved the lantern, lit the candle with the flint she kept nearby, and hastened once again into the cellar. Transferring the apples to the bushel basket, Mem shivered, this time with the understanding that while Papa had given her the farm and the orchard, it was up to her to keep them profitable—not only for herself, but for her nieces after her. Get the crop harvested and sold. Receive the money that would see her through the winter and spring. All of which would only happen after the greenings had been plucked from branches. And as of yet, she had barely cleared one tree.

Back out in the light of day, Mem stared in the direction of the road, the path the little thieves had travelled. Annoyance gave way to wistful fantasy. A sudden vision of her own sons climbing among the treetops appeared in her mind, their laughter ringing across the acres of land passed down through the generations, sun-browned legs churning in a game of hide-

and-seek. A whole family working together, as she and her sister had with their parents.

Foolishness! Mem stalked back into the orchard, chiding herself for entertaining dreams never meant to be hers. A family required a man. A trustworthy one. And those, she had learned, did not grow on any nearby tree.

No, she'd manage alone. Or wait for her nieces to grow up a bit.

Mem secured the ladder against another tree, but from the corner of her eye spied a figure coming up the road. A top hat and wide-shouldered jacket above a pair of trousers. A male visitor. Every muscle in her body tightened, reminding her of that which never long left her mind: She was a woman alone. Vulnerable. In body and reputation. She glanced down at the lantern still in her hand, fingers tightening on the handle. If she swung it hard at a man's head, it might provide enough of a stun for her to escape. Perhaps.

Just as her imagination caught hold of the idea, the man lifted his arm and waved. Mem squinted to see the face now coming into view.

Graham Lott.

Relief.

And then annoyance.

"Miss Wilkins!" He hurried forward until he stood within an arm span of her, his hat set at a rakish angle, a prodigious amount of ruffles on the cravat beneath his chin. Though he sported the fashion of a dandy, he didn't quite have the youth required to complete the look. Unless she missed her guess, he had fifty years to his credit. Twenty beyond her own three decades of existence.

"Mr. Lott." Mem dipped with her head and knees as he bent quickly from the waist. Then she had no choice but to give him her attention.

Mr. Lott didn't speak. Not at first. Instead, he surveyed the sturdy trees spreading out around them before his gaze roamed behind her, to the old stone house. Only after taking stock of the property did his eyes meet hers.

"I came to see how you were getting on with the apples, as your dear father asked me to." His mouth slid into the self-satisfied grin that turned her insides cold as ice before they steamed to a boil of fury.

"I'm managing well, sir. But thank you for thinking of me. Now if you'll pardon, I must see to my orchard while daylight remains." She gave him another quick curtsy, hoping he'd take the dismissal graciously, although he never had before. Sure enough, he followed her though the trees, finally capturing her arms and stilling her beneath the canopy of leaves.

"You're clearing the trees on your own?" He let go of her then, circled the nearest tree, *tsking* with every step.

Mem sighed, lifted one hand, and rubbed the back of her neck. "I worked beside Papa all my life and oversaw much of the business while he was ill." Not quite the same thing as picking the apples by herself, but she brushed aside that bit of truth. She would find a way to get the crop in and prove to Mr. Lott—and everyone else—she could manage alone.

"But Miss Wilkins—Remembrance—there is no need for you to be a solitary soldier. Not when I have offered to take care of everything for you. You need only to consent to be my wife." He took hold of her hand while speaking in the condescending tone she'd come to know so well in the past six months. A tone he'd never used with her when Papa was alive. In those days, he'd simply been Papa's friend. But once they had committed Papa to the ground and the fact of her inheritance had become known around town, Mr. Lott had come boldly in pursuit of her, seeming to assume Mem's affection as his due. Affection she didn't hold for him.

How could she? He'd never asked anything about her interior life—her hopes and dreams and hurts and fears, what resided inside her head and heart. She hadn't hesitated to declare her disinterest in joining herself to him. But while he'd respected her enough to back away from public pursuit, he tended to materialize from the shadows the minute she found herself alone. Alone in town, at least. He hadn't sought her at the farm before. Not until today.

She gently slipped her hand free of his grasp and took a step backward, praying he would take the hint and leave. "Thank you, Mr. Lott, for your . . . concern, but I believe I have made myself clear in the past and will continue to assert that while I am honored at what you have offered, I am quite determined to remain as I am. I have everything under control."

No need for him to know she did not. She simply had to behave as if she did.

He stood silent for a long moment, then tipped his had and bid her good day. Her knees shook as he walked away, unsure what she would have done if he'd persisted. But she had to make him understand that she had no intention of giving up her independence. Not for him. Not for any man.

Papa may have believed stubbornness her besetting sin, but he was wrong. Her stubbornness would be her only salvation. For if the orchard did not succeed, she feared the consequences would be unbearable.

CHAPTER 2

"Hurry, Timothy." Simon Brennan tugged his four-year-old son's hand, determined to meet with one more building owner before the sun slipped beneath the horizon.

"But my feet hurt, Da," Timothy whined from behind.

Simon frowned. Of course the lad's feet ached. Because the cobbler's son was always the last to get a new pair of shoes. He'd made sure Timothy's shoes fit when they'd left Dublin six weeks ago, but the boy had grown on the voyage over. Simon could see the evidence in Timothy's skeleton suit, the sleeves no longer meeting his wrists, the trousers rising above his ankles. But before he could fashion a new pair of shoes for the lad—and commission larger clothing—he had to find a place for them both. A place to work. And to live.

Simon shortened his stride, slowed his pace. Still his son remained behind, dragging his feet along the dusty street, resisting his father's pull. Simon's jaw tightened. He'd thought the boy would relish the exercise of the day after being confined on a ship for so many weeks. Apparently, he was mistaken.

He turned, ready to chide his son for ill behavior, but the slumped shoulders, the dimpled chin resting against the narrow chest, imprisoned Simon's words. Timothy was but a child, after all. A boy who'd left the only home he'd ever known to be set aground in a strange place.

Simon stopped and squatted in front of the lad, put a finger beneath the boy's chin and lifted his face. Black, curly hair curtained Timothy's deep blue eyes—eyes that mirrored his mother's, God rest her soul. Simon looked away and swallowed hard. Nearly two years gone, and still the ache remained.

He stood, set his hand atop his son's head. "Just a wee bit longer, lad. I promise. Mr. Archibald's building might be just the place we've been searchin' for."

"Can't I wait here?" Timothy plopped down in the scrubby grass between two buildings—one brick, one clapboard.

"You cannot." Simon picked up his son. Timothy stiffened, calling Simon's impatience even nearer the surface. Then a new idea struck. "But you may sit here."

Before Timothy could protest, Simon swung the lad above his head then settled the boy's bum on the back of his neck, one spindly leg over each of his shoulders. "Better?"

Timothy's thin arms reached down and circled Simon's face in a quick squeeze before his hands settled atop Simon's head. "Go, Da! Go!" Small heels drummed against Simon's chest, pretending him a horse in need of a gallop.

Simon strode forward, grateful for the sound of laughter over complaint, praying Mr. Archibald's free space might fit his needs—and his pocketbook. Just a small storefront in which to make and sell his shoes, with a room behind for sleeping and simple cooking. Two men alone didn't require many comforts.

A few minutes later, Simon approached a wooden structure on the north side of the street. Third from the end, painted yellow, or so said Isaac Hyer, proprietor of the Gray Goose. Simon peered through a moderate-sized plate of glass into the empty room. He couldn't see much, but it seemed ample enough. And the window would provide a place to display his craftsmanship. He stepped back and looked up. No placard hung above the door, but he could manage that, too.

There were other cobblers in Providence. He knew that. He'd passed their establishments. Even spoken with a few. But the town was expanding, the population booming now that the war with Britain was over. And every resident needed shoes. Enough trade for many men, especially one who worked hard and knew how to hold on to his money. Here he wouldn't need help to provide for his son—or receive interference in raising him.

Please, God. He hadn't words for more than that simple plea. If this building had been let or cost too dear, he'd need to find someone to watch Timothy tomorrow while he made more inquiries. Four-year-old legs hadn't the stamina for another long day of fruitless walking. Simon swung Timothy to the ground, clasped the lad's hand, and pushed open the door.

Walls the color of soot, as if the chimney hadn't enough draw, framed the square space. But chimneys could be repaired and walls washed. Simon stepped into the room, lingering dust choking his throat and drawing water into his eyes. He turned to the window that overlooked the street. At least it let in some light. He peered though a doorway opposite the window, into the space behind. A small room, fireplace at one end. The perfect space for them to sleep and eat. Yes, this building would do, as long as the price was right. He simply needed to find Mr. Archibald and discuss the particulars.

Simon let go of his son's hand. Timothy crisscrossed the floor at a run, his feet suddenly less painful than before. Hands fisted on his waist, Simon surveyed the room again. Hyer said Archibald often spent his days here, that he was anxious to secure a tenant to enable him to go live with his daughter. So where was he? Simon turned in a circle, as if he'd missed the man standing in the empty room. Only he hadn't. And judging from the undisturbed dust on the floor, no one had been inside in a while.

Simon glanced outside at the violet sky. They ought to return to the Gray Goose for a hot meal before claiming their spots on the floor of a common sleeping room. He could return in the morning, when he had time to wait. Or time to search out the absentee owner.

"Let's go." Simon reached for Timothy's hand.

Timothy laughed, sprinted beyond Simon's reach.

"Timothy." The name came out like a growl, Simon's patience as frayed as the end of a well-used rope.

With another giggle, Timothy ran toward the door, the one leading to the street. At least he was headed in the right direction. Simon followed with long strides. But just as Timothy set his hand on the latch, the door swung open. Timothy stumbled backward, his feet tangling with one another. Simon caught him just before he hit the floor.

"Who are you and what are you doing here?" The middle-aged man dressed in silk pantaloons and coat punctuated the question with a tap of his walking stick on the wooden floor.

Bile rose up Simon's throat. He'd seen such dandies before. The kind who wanted to squash men like Simon under their polished Hessian boots. Men he'd thought he'd escape in America.

He couldn't afford to antagonize this kind of man. Not yet.

Simon swallowed his pride, removed his hat and lowered his gaze as he stepped in front of Timothy, shielding him from the man's disdain. "Simon Brennan, Mr. Archibald. I'm a shoemaker, just arrived from—"

"Archibald?" The man shook his head. "Phineas Archibald doesn't own this place anymore. I do."

Simon clenched his teeth to hold in a retort, pinning his gaze to a place on the floor. He hoped the man would take his action for deference instead of what it really was—an attempt to hide his seething anger. "I'm sorry, sir. Mr. Hyer at the Gray Goose said Mr. Archibald was looking for a tenant, and I—"

"Have you any silver?"

Simon jerked his head up. The man's gaze roamed him up then down, as if attempting to surmise the fullness—or emptiness—of his trouser pockets.

Simon pulled his shoulders back, stood straighter. "Aye, sir. British pounds. In bank notes. Lately arrived from Dublin, we are. Me and th' lad." Simon drew Timothy around to stand in front of him, hating himself for using the boy to attempt to soften the landlord. "We're ready for a new start, so if you'll tell me how much for the rooms, Mr … ?"

"Lott. Graham Lott." The man clasped his hands behind his back and crossed in front of the window. "Bank notes won't do. Silver dollars. Spanish milled, preferably. One-fifty a year. First year's payment due before you move in."

One hundred and fifty silver dollars? Where would he get that kind of money? Simon rested his shaking hands on Timothy's shoulders. He hadn't planned for such an amount. Not with food and materials still to be bought before he'd see paying customers. Perhaps he could barter for part of the payment. He looked down at Mr. Lott's boots, but the pristine leather told him the man had no need of his services.

"Yes? No?"

Simon shook his head. "Thank ye, Mr. Lott, for your time."

He'd have to find another way. And he'd have to find it soon. Every day at the Gray Goose ate away at the store of cash he'd brought from Ireland. And he refused to have made the trip across the ocean only to find himself at the bottom of the heap once more.

CHAPTER 3

STIFLING. That's what Mem thought as she reached the edge of town to find the morning sun spilling over brick buildings rising up out of the earth and people swarming to and fro like ants around a dropped crust of bread. Already she wished herself back among her peaceful grove of trees, even if their hanging fruit mocked her.

She'd fallen asleep over her supper last evening, exhausted, after clearing only two trees. Two. Out of two hundred. So much to do, and yet she found herself in town because she was worried over Charity. Her conscience would be appeased by nothing less than a short visit to set her mind at ease. At least she hoped it would be short.

A deep groan of premonition wound its way out of her belly, a noise lost in the cacophony of town. Waves lapping. Birds calling. Voices shouting. Wood creaking. Horseshoes ringing and wheels rumbling over cobblestoned streets. Why Isaac and Charity preferred living in the middle of this bustle, she would never know. But while she didn't understand them, she appreciated that at their marriage they'd taken the gift of Papa's savings with the knowledge that Mem would then receive the farm. For that, she was grateful. For as much as she loved her sister, brother-in-law, and three small nieces, she didn't know if she'd feel the same about them should she have to live with them every day.

She had her own work. Her own home. Her own source of income. Mem smiled, imagining Mr. Ivey, Papa's factor, counting silver coins into her hand. Money to see her through another cycle of seasons in which her fruit would sprout, grow, ripen. The thought sent her spirit soaring higher than the sea birds circling the docks. The joy reached all the way to her toes, making her wish to run unhindered the last block of her journey.

Instead, she waited serenely for two horse carts to pass before crossing Westminster Street at a sedate and steady pace. A breeze kicked up from over the ocean, and by the time she reached the Gray Goose, the painted wooden sign over its door rocked back and forth as if waving visitors inside.

Mem took a deep breath and crossed the threshold. It always took her aback, this immediate absence of sunshine. She blinked, then scanned the shadowy room for Isaac, finally spotting him by the length of counter near the stairs. In conversation with someone. She squinted. Someone she didn't recognize.

Strangers were not unusual here, certainly. After all, Providence was a port town, and the Gray Goose attracted many a traveler, as well as a steady stream of politicians. Isaac had gained quite a reputation with both, as his dining room often boasted a number of the leading merchants and craftsmen of Providence. It also hosted their often rowdy political discussions.

She hurried across the room. No need to interrupt or linger for a greeting. Charity and the girls would be upstairs, on the third floor, their family rooms nestled beneath the gabled roof. Rooms with windows ushering in abundant air and light. Rooms housing three small girls and Charity, who waited to be delivered of her fourth child.

With one foot on the stairs, Mem glanced over at Isaac, but

found the stranger's gaze locked onto hers instead. A man near to her own age. Taller than Isaac. Hair black as night curling about his ears and coat collar. His attention remained on her a shade longer than appropriate. Heat crawled up her neck as her eyes sought her feet and she tried to quiet the sudden tumult in her stomach.

"Mem!" Isaac's voice boomed into the silence. He clasped her hands and led her off the stairs before pressing a brotherly kiss to her cheek. "So glad you're here." He stepped back to include the stranger in the conversation. "Have the pleasure to meet Simon Brennan, a recent émigré to our fair land. He and his son have taken space in one of our rooms. Mr. Brennan, my sister-in-law, Remembrance Wilkins."

Mem dropped into a quick curtsy, head bent toward the floor. She refused to be undone by a well-appointed face, as she had before. But as her gaze sought a different resting place, it snagged on the man's hands. Broad, strong. Not scarred by heavy toil or lily white from lack of use. As if his labor was both strong and soft at the same time. Curiosity nipped like a puppy at her heels. What had brought this man to America's shores? And why did she care to know?

"Mrs. Wilkins." He tipped his hat then excused himself from their conversation. Before Mem could force her thoughts from the stranger—let alone correct his mistaken assumption as to her marital status—he departed the establishment, leaving her with an uncharacteristic weakness in her knees.

Isaac reached for her cloak, his voice pulling her thoughts back to the familiar. "Annie fell hauling in water from the well. Her knee swelled like a blowfish before half an hour had passed. I sent her home, but now I'm without help for the busy hours." His eyebrows rose, asking the question he left unvoiced.

Mem winced. He knew how much she hated serving in the dining room. The work didn't bother her. It was the expected interaction with customers. Small talk didn't come easily, not even with those she'd known her entire life. Unlike Isaac and

Charity, who both thrived on conversation with anyone, anywhere, anytime. But Charity had been retired to her rooms for two months already. She couldn't help, even if she wanted to. And Isaac wouldn't have asked Mem if he weren't desperate.

Mem hid her sigh behind a small exhale before forcing herself to smile into Isaac's hopeful face. "Of course, I'll help. I'll be upstairs with the girls. Call when you need me."

His grin was her reward. "Just the busy times, Mem. I promise. Noon, then supper." He disappeared out the side door, off to the kitchen enclosure behind the building.

So much for a short visit, Mem thought as she climbed the stairs, grimacing at the ordeal that awaited her at mealtimes and the hours away from the farm she hadn't anticipated. Still, she didn't mind being of help. She appreciated Isaac's friendship— and his love for her sister. Beyond Papa, Isaac's was the only example of masculine faithfulness Mem trusted. A reputation earned over ten long years, and one especially sweet in the light of his older brother's betrayal.

Passing the guest rooms on the second floor—two common, two private—she headed up to the top of the building. A high-pitched squeal preceded the patter of small feet across wooden floors. Mem pushed open the parlor door. Three young girls— all still in night dress—stopped scampering and stared. Then they rushed at her, voices shouting in unison.

"Auntie Mem! Auntie Mem!" Tiny hands clutched at her skirt. Skinny arms reached up to circle her waist. She kissed five-year-old Grace's head, stooped to rub noses with three-year-old Agnes, and lifted the baby, Clara, almost a year old, into her arms. Then she noticed the little boy sitting by himself in the corner.

"And who do we have here?" She knelt in front of the child, his tear-stained face plucking at her heartstrings.

"Tim'thy," he sniffled, running his sleeve under his nose.

"He's staying to play with us today," Grace announced with a grin.

Mem handed Clara into Grace's open arms and bent closer to the forlorn boy. "Maybe you can help me corral these rowdy girls." She winked, hoping to draw him into her game.

With a shy grin, he heaved himself off the floor and clutched Mem's outstretched hand.

"And where is Mamma?" Mem sing-songed to her nieces, hoping the tone would soothe the girls as well as beckoned her sister.

"I'm here." The muffled reply from the adjoining bedroom preceded Charity's shuffle into view, her stomach arriving well before the rest of her. At least she wore clothing, of sorts. A rumpled dress billowed about her extended middle as she tried to tie behind her the ribbon that would gather the fabric beneath her rounded breasts. "If this baby doesn't come soon …"

Mem let go of Timothy and met Charity in the center of the room. She wrapped her arms around her sister's shoulders and pulled her in as close as she could for a hug, hoping to dispel some of Charity's gloom. "If this baby doesn't come soon, you'll wait until it does." Mem pulled away and kissed Charity's cheek. "Good morning, sister."

Charity grinned, but it didn't last long. Mem urged her toward the long settee on the far wall. "I'm here for the day, apparently, since Isaac needs my help serving." She cut her eyes to the boy—Timothy—nestled near her skirt. "And I think you need help here, too."

"What happened downstairs?" Charity stretched her legs along the length of the settee. Mem couldn't help but notice the puffiness of her sister's usually shapely ankles.

"Apparently Annie's hurt her knee and hobbled home. I'm just needed during the busy hours."

Charity groaned. "I'm so sorry, Mem. I know you hate that. If I could just—" she set her feet on the floor, but Mem shook her head, glaring until her sister returned to her reclining position.

"You can't. I can. I'll get the girls dressed and tidy up a bit. Then maybe you won't feel so ..." Mem wasn't sure what word to use, for she really had no idea how Charity felt. She could imagine, but she didn't know.

Charity leaned her head back against the settee and shut her eyes. "Thank you, Mem."

Mem put a finger to her lips and led the girls and their new companion from the room.

CHAPTER 4

Simon's stomach rumbled, reminding him he'd eaten nothing since before the sun rose. And still he was no closer to securing a spot to live and work. He looked up at an ale house, but chose to pass on by. He'd track down Mr. Lott before returning to the Gray Goose for supper. He had no desire to patronize any other establishment. Not after Isaac Hyer offered use of his name as a reference with the men of business about town. And indeed, Hyer's name had gained him entrance and credibility, even if none of the men had what he needed—or could afford.

He'd left Timothy in the care of Hyer's very pregnant wife. An uneasy compromise, for certain. But all he had. He'd hoped God would answer his morning prayers of a place for them to settle. A place to live out the life he and Alannah had dreamed for their family.

But now, after discovering yet another suitable building already spoken for, he wondered. Perhaps God hadn't meant them to stay here at all. If needs must, they could move farther inland, seek some larger town. Simon peered into the September sky, squinting at the brightness of the waning sun, listening to sea birds scold the men busy on the docks. When he lowered his gaze earthward, tall evergreens framed the glittering blue ocean on the horizon.

He didn't want to leave here. Less than a week and already it felt more like home than the Emerald Isle.

Perspiration dripped down the side of Simon's face as he banished thoughts of the old country, his old life, from his head. But Gerald Kavanagh's face rose in his mind anyway. Alannah's father. A man with a little land, no title, and a strut more arrogant than a banty rooster. No better than Simon, for sure and certain. But he thought himself so. Made that clear in words to Simon that never reached Alannah's ears. Kavanagh loved his only daughter and gave into her pleas for his blessing of her marriage. But that didn't mean he liked it. Or that he accepted Simon into their family.

Years of skewering words—those of Kavanagh and others—sliced through Simon, making his steps heavier, his stride longer. His trade provided well enough, even if it hadn't afforded him a plot of land in his name. And it had given him clout in the town, no matter what men like Kavanagh thought.

Simon's hands became fists, alerting him to the anger he'd allowed to boil over. It brought him to a halt. He relaxed his fingers. Shook his head. How had he allowed Gerald Kavanagh to stir his blood even here? Distance from him was the reason he'd pushed Alannah to agree to cross the ocean. *In America,* he'd said, *we can buy land that will be ours, not your da's. We can be our own family.* A plan he'd determined to make happen even after the Irish soil became her permanent resting place. Here, no one would hover over Timothy, acting as if Simon couldn't raise his son properly.

Simon's chin dropped to his chest as his hands landed on his hips. He blew out a long breath, hoping to relieve the ache. He'd not only thought to escape Kavanagh's shadow in America, he'd also thought to hide from sorrow, be free from memories of Alannah lurking around every corner.

But he'd been wrong. Even with hope for the future, Simon felt incomplete. Untethered.

Alone.

He clenched his teeth, his jaw screwing tighter as another grumble from his gut stirred thoughts of the filling fare at the Gray Goose—and brought Isaac Hyer's sister-in-law to mind unbidden. Not a strikingly beautiful face, but something in it had captured his interest. The intelligent glint in her eye? The confident set of her mouth? Or the blush that stole across her cheeks at his attention? Simon shook the vision away. Married to a local farmer, no doubt. And with a passel of offspring to her credit.

He squared his shoulders, straightened his hat, and brushed the dust from his coat. No more time to waste thinking of the past—or the future. He needed to secure the present. He wouldn't give up. Not yet. He'd find Mr. Lott again, work out a plan agreeable to them both. Then he and Timothy could settle into their new life.

Simon turned his feet toward Mr. Lott's building, enjoying the cool that came with the shady side of the street. Two more blocks south, if he remembered correctly. Mr. Lott hadn't impressed on their first meeting. Too similar to Kavanagh for Simon's liking. But Simon wasn't seeking to marry the man's daughter. Only rent his building. Surely that could be accomplished without rancor.

This time, Simon rapped on the door instead of entering. No answer. He pressed his face to the window, cupping his hands to see inside.

Empty, just as before.

Rubbing the back of his neck, he wondered what step to take next. Noises from his middle settled the question. Return to the Gray Goose. Come back here at dawn and wait until the man showed himself.

As Simon turned to go, a door opened in the adjacent building. An elderly man hobbled outside.

"Excuse me, sir." Simon moved closer to the man, ready to catch him if he toppled over. "Would ye happen to know the whereabouts of a Mr. Lott? I'd like to inquire about his buildin'."

The man's eyes crinkled into slits. "Not from around here, are you?"

"No, sir. Simon Brennan, lately of County Carlow." He stuck out his hand, but the old man simply stared at it. Then nodded toward the door he'd just exited.

"Lott's in there." The man jabbed his thumb over his shoulder as he shook his head. "But he's in a surly mood." He shuffled past Simon, then stopped and looked back. "Might as well try as not."

Simon took a deep breath. Was this God's way of smiling on him? His tired feet found a more sprightly step as he made his way to Lott's office.

Fifteen minutes later, he left with no more liking for the man, but a verbal agreement about the empty building at a price Simon could live with. To meet the rent would require almost all the silver he could acquire with his store of British pounds, but he was no stranger to hard work, and he and Timothy had few needs. They'd survive and more. Of that he was sure. For he already felt a kinship with the people of this new country, who'd bested the British in two wars no one gave them a chance of winning.

Simon swiped his palms against one another, as if wiping the final dust of Ireland from his hands. He would be an American now. Free to make his fortune. Just as he and Alannah had dreamed.

CHAPTER 5

MEM USED her sleeve to wipe the moisture from her forehead, then pressed her hands into the small of her back and stretched. A long day. The children had kept her moving upstairs, the customers downstairs. She wanted to sink into Mama and Papa's big box bed and sleep until after sunrise. But she couldn't. Not with supper to be served, apples to harvest, and Charity's babe about to appear.

Mem didn't mind helping out, but she didn't have time to serve every meal for days on end. Annie's knee needed to heal quickly. Mem hoped they'd thought to put a comfrey cloth on it, reduce the swelling and bring her back to work soon.

Hands full of used plates and cups, Mem stopped at a newly occupied table, her mood suddenly brightening.

"Timothy!" She held the soiled dishes aloft as the boy leapt from his chair and threw his arms around her waist. His small cheek pressed into her side and warmed her inside and out.

"Timothy." The stern tone caused Mem's heart to thump in recognition. The man from this morning, with his intense gaze and strong hands.

Mr . . . Brennan.

Her gaze skittered between him and Timothy, noting the similarity of their features. Father and son, definitely. Her smile widened. "What can I bring you to eat?"

Mr. Brennan blinked slowly, as if weighing her words.

"Hurry, Da! I'm hungry!" Timothy bounced in his seat. Mem held her breath, expecting gruffness, but Mr. Brennan's expression fell into more pleasant lines as he looked at his son, then up at her. "Whatever you deem best from the kitchen this evening." The interest in his gaze set her face ablaze.

He's new here, she reminded herself. He wouldn't realize she wasn't a normal serving girl. Or a woman who men generally noticed. At least not anymore. Not since the bloom of her youth had begun to fade.

Not that it wasn't nice to be noticed. And by a handsome man, at that. But hard experience had taught her that handsome men weren't necessarily trustworthy ones.

"I'd choose rabbit stew," Mem mumbled, ready to flee into the obscurity of the kitchen.

Timothy tugged at her sleeve, demanding attention. She focused on him, ignoring his father with a deftness honed by betrayal. And age.

"Me, too, Miss Mem."

She crouched down, peered into the boy's eyes. "Auntie Mem, remember?"

He nodded with vigor.

"Don't worry, I'll make sure you don't go to bed hungry." She wished her hands weren't full and she could tousle the boy's hair, even kiss the top of his head. In the few hours he'd played with her nieces today, he'd poked holes in the bastions around her heart. Still, she'd not make the same concessions to his father, no matter how pleasing his face.

She returned with two pewter plates filled with steaming stew, her heart turning over at Mr. Brennan's kind gaze. Thereafter, on every trip through the dining room, she glanced his direction. Mr. Brennan seemed less serious now. More relaxed as he cut the chunks of meat in Timothy's dish into smaller portions and laughed at something his son had said. Was it the love for his child that transformed him? The thought consumed her as completely as fog on a spring morning, but she forced it away, having no desire to nourish a hope sure to disappoint.

As she picked up their empty plates, Mr. Brennan wiped Timothy's mouth with his handkerchief.

"Did you ever know a lad to put more supper on his face than in his belly, Mrs. Wilkins?"

"It's—I'm *Miss* Wilkins." Mem's face heated as the words rushed from her lips. But Mr. Brennan had spoken as if they were long time acquaintances rather than practically strangers, so it seemed only fitting to correct his mistake. After all, she *had* told his son to call her Auntie Mem, so she'd actually been the one to begin the intimacy.

"*Miss* Wilkins." The slow smile that bloomed on his face set her stomach fluttering. He leaned back in his chair, appraising her unapologetically now. "At least my son and I will soon have supper in front of our own fire and spare the public this spectacle."

"You're leaving?" Mem hated the breathy way her question emerged, as if his leaving had anything to do with her.

"Aye. The inn, at least. I've found a spot to settle, to make shoes and raise my lad." He tousled Timothy's hair as the boy giggled.

Shoes. He made shoes. She thought again of his hands. Strong yet soft, just as needed to manipulate heavy leathers and more delicate fabrics. She pulled back her skirt to reveal her own feet, now throbbing. A new pair of pumps wouldn't come amiss. Perhaps after she sold the crop she could engage Mr. Brennan's services.

But she couldn't think about that now. She still had supper service to complete. And apples to harvest.

"Very good to hear, sir. We look forward to seeing you and your son in our fair city." Suddenly uncomfortable beneath his gaze, she whisked their dishes from the table and bolted for the kitchen.

LONG AFTER MR. BRENNAN and Timothy had left the dining room, after most chairs were empty and the hot food all but gone, a gentle hand fell on her shoulder. She turned.

Isaac grinned, looking as fresh as if he'd come off a good night's sleep. "I'll find someone to take you home, Mem. I know you need your fresh air—and quiet."

She nodded, Isaac's face blurring through a sheen of tears. Oh, how well he knew her!

"I'll say good-bye to Charity, first." She put her foot to the stairs, in spite of the exhaustion that weighed on her every limb. When she returned to the dining room, she grabbed her cloak from a peg on the wall and wrapped it around her shoulders. As she tied the ribbon beneath her chin, Isaac appeared again.

"Mr. Brennan assured me it would be no trouble."

"Mr. Brennan?" Her stomach twirled, and her knees shimmied. Why on earth would Isaac ask *him* to convey her home? Before she could protest, the man himself appeared, hat in hand, broad smile plastered across his face, accentuating two dimples she'd not noticed before.

That smile. Much more free than any he'd put on display earlier, even in Timothy's presence. Her legs went flimsy as fresh jelly.

"Of course. Thank you, Mr. Brennan. I appreciate—"

"If I may, Miss Wilkins." Graham Lott sidled between Mem and Mr. Brennan, bending over her hand in such a way that Mr. Brennan had to move backward. "I hear you are in need of a ride home. I would be happy to render you such a service."

Mem looked from Mr. Brennan to Mr. Lott then back again. Her smile faltered, realizing Isaac had left her alone with them. What was she to say now? If only Mr. Brennan would understand her pleading gaze. Instead, Mr. Brennan nodded, his expression suddenly void of softness.

"I see you're in capable hands, Miss Wilkins." Then he mounted the stairs and disappeared from sight.

Mem's heart sank, but she couldn't expect him to understand her predicament. And right now she longed only to be at home. She forced herself to smile, in spite of Mr. Lott's smugness. "Shall we go, then?"

Mr. Lott escorted her to his curricle and helped her to the seat. The horses tossed their heads, eager to be on the road. Once they left the confines of town, Mem drew in a deep breath and raised her gaze to the night sky. Clouds covered the slice of moon and the usually bright stars, leaving her to again remember Simon Brennan's fathomless dark eyes.

Confusion fluttered through her breast, sending her eyebrows dipping toward her nose and stretching her mouth into a frown. That Irishman had no right to interrupt her thoughts. She hadn't invited him in. Though she didn't find the intrusion as unwelcome as she ought.

"They work you too hard," Mr. Lott said, reminding Mem she wasn't alone.

Her heart crawled up her throat as she remembered the determination in Mr. Lott's eyes when he'd stepped around Mr. Brennan. In spite of her refusal of his attentions yesterday, she wasn't quit of him yet.

She sighed, hoping he'd attribute it to the strain of the day instead of her exasperation with his presence. She had no desire to antagonize him, even if she wouldn't gratify his desire.

"My sister and brother-in-law are masters of a kindly nature." Her words held a bit of wicked humor behind them, but she doubted Mr. Lott would recognize such. Not from a woman.

As she expected, his beady eyes squinted at her in confusion. "Masters? But you are always such an advocate of the independent life."

Mem's laughter sailed away in the gusty current. "Indeed, Mr. Lott. But on occasion there is a Christian duty to serve those we love and those in need. How much more so when they are one in the same person?"

Mr. Lott leaned his shoulder nearer to hers. "But who shall see to your needs, Miss Wilkins? That is my concern."

Mem shrugged. "As you know, I have few needs that I cannot care for on my own."

"So you have no concern for your apples? No need for help with the harvest?"

She flinched—and hated herself for it. But his words stung like needle grass working its way through stockings and finding flesh. She did need help. She just didn't want it. Didn't want to be beholden. Especially to him. But she had to get the crop in. And as much as she wanted to deny it, that would require help of some sort. Perhaps his concern did arise from his friendship with her father. After all, she hadn't been coy about her feelings. Perhaps her pride was standing in the way of the Lord's provision.

She forced the words past her lips. "Yes, I do need help."

Mr. Lott's chest seemed to puff out farther than normal. "And that, my lady, is why I am here." He rested a hand on her arm for a short moment before returning it to the reins. "Have no fear. I will take your crop in hand—and get you the best price possible."

The eagerness in his eyes, the fleeting nature of his touch persuaded her of his sincerity. She needed to stop being so suspicious of his motives, trust that his help came from a place of friendship and Christian love. So she nodded, ignoring the tumult inside her.

"Thank you, Mr. Lott. You have removed a great weight from my mind. I am grateful for the opportunity to give myself to Isaac and Charity and their children as they need me."

"As you should, my dear. As you should." He pulled the horses to a gentle stop in front of her home. Once he'd helped her down, he accompanied her to the door. "If you'll allow me, I'll return in the morning to carry you back to the Gray Goose. Then we can discuss our arrangement in further detail."

As much as she longed to refuse, Mem knew the only appropriate answer was yes.

CHAPTER 6

"AND SO YOU REFUSED HIM AGAIN?" Charity sorted through her family's clothing looking for mending that needed done while Mem continued to clean—the floor, the windows, anything the girls had touched in an attempt to avoid the coming conversation. She almost wished now that she hadn't told Charity of her arrangement with Mr. Lott. But she hadn't much choice. Not when Charity had seen Mem arrive with him this morning.

"I didn't have to. As I said, this time he offered his help, but this time he didn't ask for my hand."

Charity shook her head. "I fear his tenacity."

As did Mem. She glanced around the room, unable to find another obviously filthy nook or cranny, so she washed her hands, smoothed her dress. Almost time for her assistance downstairs. She turned to her sister. "As much as I hate to admit it, Charity, I do need help, especially if I'm to be with you these next few weeks."

"Oh, Mem!" Charity extended her hand. Mem took it, squeezed, then continued to ready herself to meet the public. Charity huffed and crossed her arms atop her protruding belly.

"It's just that I don't trust that wrinkled old peacock. I never have."

"Me, either. But I haven't any other choice, do I?" Mem regretted the petulance in her voice the moment Charity's mouth quivered. She softened her tone. "If you need me, send one of the girls down."

Charity waved her away, though a frown still sat on her face. "I'm fine. No need to worry."

But Mem did worry. She didn't like the pasty color of Charity's face, the twitch of her jaw indicating she was lying. Or at least not telling the entire truth. Each of her babies had come more quickly than the last, meaning there would likely be little time to fetch Mrs. Gladstone, the midwife. Perhaps she ought to stay the night, forego Mr. Lott's offer to drive her home each evening.

"Humor your big sister." Mem forced a smile and waited for Charity's nod before hurrying down to the kitchen.

The warmth of the large hearth engulfed her, the supper hour already in full sway. Mrs. Allen, a wiry negro woman, bustled about the room, one eye on her cooking pot, one on her teenaged son, Wilson, who stood over a wooden tub washing dishes.

"Everything all right upstairs?" Isaac passed by her as he spoke, leaving no time for an answer. Mem shrugged at Mrs. Allen, who smiled back and shook her head.

Picking up two full plates from the large table in the center of the room, Mem readied herself for another round of serving. At least she'd had her encounter with Graham Lott for the day. She wouldn't be on edge, wondering when he would appear. That was some consolation. And she had to admit his offer of help had been a generous one. To take her crop in hand for no fee. An offer unaccompanied by another proposal of marriage, too. Perhaps he'd actually taken her refusals as truth.

Relief. Finally.

But alongside relief came another feeling, a less understandable one.

Dissatisfaction.

In the dining room, two men from her church congregation signaled to her from a back table. She raised her chin in acknowledgement and made her way to them, set a steaming rabbit pie before each one. As tables filled and emptied, she traversed the floor serving food and drink, engaging an occasional word of greeting. Her limbs felt limp as wet rags, but she refused to waver. She wasn't some fine lady unused to difficult work. She simply wasn't used to this variety of work. She much preferred her crops to Isaac's customers.

Back in the kitchen, her uncomfortable thought returned. Why should she be discontent? Was it Mr. Lott's offer of help— or the fact that it came from him? But who else would propose such assistance? None but a man determined to wrench her inheritance from her hands, to gain control of her land through marriage. But in spite of this knowledge, when she glanced at Isaac, the disquiet in her swelled. If only there were another like him. A trustworthy man who viewed his wife as a partner, their life together as more than a business arrangement.

She re-entered the dining room, her gaze sweeping the tables, noting faces familiar and foreign, but not the one she was loathe to admit she wanted to see. Was she, like Charity, not speaking the entire truth of the matter? Maybe, just maybe, her heart did still believe there might be someone good and faithful and true. Someone who would love her for who she was, not what she possessed.

Or didn't possess.

Maybe.

SIMON AND TIMOTHY slipped into the Gray Goose, both ready for a hearty meal after a long day spent gathering the coin needed for Mr. Lott, tracking down the man again, procuring the key, and moving their few belongings to the building that would be their home. Now Simon intended to enjoy the success of the day with his son, to celebrate with one more sumptuous meal before the simplicity of cooking at his own fire.

Timothy clutched his hand as they crossed the room to an open table. A few men nodded at him in acquaintance, sealing his attachment to Providence and its burgeoning prosperity. The cotton mills established during the latest war with Britain contributed to that, as did, of course, the bountiful farms dotting the countryside. And the port thrived with the war's end, as well. Commerce from all parts of the world. A growing population. And all—every one—would need shoes to cover their feet. Shoes that would need replacing over time. A never-ending business that would fill his days and his pocketbook. Allow him to see to Timothy's education and future.

If only Alannah could dream with him over the coming success. If only he could see her eyes light with gratitude when he supplied her with the things she'd thought sacrificed in her love of a simple man. Things common in her father's home, but not in Simon's. But some things could not be. No use to dwell on them.

Issac Hyer set a tankard of ale in front of him, a cup of cider in front of his son. "All settled?"

"Settled indeed." Simon held up his glass as in a toast before letting the ale soothe his parched throat.

"Splendid. Though my girls will miss having Timothy to brighten their days." Isaac grinned, slapped the tabletop as if signaling his need to move on. "I'll will be along shortly with your supper."

Simon frowned but nodded as he set the tankard gently on the stained wooden table. He'd hoped—perhaps unreasonably —that Miss Wilkins would attend that chore. In fact, it might have been the very reason for his decision to put forth more coin he oughtn't spare when they could very well have supped on a pot of porridge or a hot potato and some bacon.

Ah, well. He'd only wanted a look at her anyway. And enjoy some conversation. Nothing more. He could survive without it.

A quick grin brightened Timothy's face. When Simon turned to find the reason, his gaze slammed into Miss Wilkins's. Her eyes danced, and his heart proclaimed he could not, indeed, survive on his own. Not completely.

"I'm so glad to see you, Mr. Brennan." She set a large plate of food between them. "And you, Timothy. I assume you were quite a help to your father—"

"Da!"

"Your *da* today." Miss Wilkins smiled at Timothy, ruffled the unruly hair on his head.

Simon couldn't dim his smile, especially when Timothy tucked into his summer and left Simon to carry on the conversation. "A help, for sure, Remembrance."

Simon stilled at her startled expression, mortified he'd spoken aloud. "I, uh . . . I just remembered your name. Your Christian name. From before." He squinted at Timothy, trying to recover from his blunder. "Mem. Miss Mem. Miss Wilkins, I mean. I didn't think—I—"

She lowered her head, removing his ability to read her face. Embarrassed for herself—or for him? Simon wanted to kick himself. To start again. To make the encounter memorable for very different reasons than it was now.

Her shoulders shook. She covered her mouth with one hand. Raised her head. Burst out laughing.

Simon smiled, but couldn't shake his earlier unease. Especially as she continued to laugh, even wiped her eyes with her apron. Finally, she glanced around and composed herself.

"I'm so sorry, Mr. Brennan. It just struck me funny. There are so few who call me by that name. But please, I prefer Mem from my friends. Everyone around here knows me as such. And, well, I guess since Timothy and I have spent a bit of time together, I'd forgotten you and I have only known each other. . .." Her words drifted into silence, her entire demeanor moving from comfort to anxiety, from humor to embarrassment. "If you'll excuse me."

Simon stood as she fled, wishing he could have caught her, told her how grateful he was that she had watched over his son. That he, too, felt they'd known each other a long time already, even if their acquaintance was but three days old. Slowly, he lowered to his seat, every muscle taut with a wild desire to pursue her, but every thought warning that he must wait. Eye and ear alert for her return, he picked up his fork and began to eat.

AFTER SUPPER, Simon remained at the table. He asked Timothy questions, listened to him talk of his antics with the Hyer girls when he'd been with them. But though his ears were attuned to his son, he couldn't tear his gaze from Miss Wilkins as she bustled about, cheeks flushed, mouth tight. Nothing like Alannah, who'd been small in stature, soft of speech. Not that Alannah was weak, but all her strength lay hidden inside her. Otherwise how would such a girl persuade her father to accept her marriage to a cobbler?

But this woman—Mem—she was different. A bundle of physical vitality, but something behind her words, something in the gentleness of her movement, spoke of vulnerability. Timothy called for his attention, but before he could remove his gaze from Mem, she stopped at a table on the other side of the room to talk with another customer. A man with his back to Simon. It was the first time he'd seen her engage in more than a few words in the progress of her work. Except with him, of course.

Not that it was any of his business.

He downed the last of his ale and forced his eyes to his son's face. But his gaze soon strayed back to her. They were still talking, Mem and the man. Except now she seemed to have stiffened, shoulders high and tight around her ears, eyes narrowed to slits.

Simon half-stood, searched the room for Hyer, sure he would step in should the customer give his sister-in-law a hard time. But Simon couldn't find him. In fact, no one seemed to notice the tense conversation happening near the door. Perhaps he ought to move closer, assure himself that the interaction was nothing more than a friendly conversation.

"Stay here," he instructed Timothy.

Just as Simon reached his feet, the man grabbed Mem's wrist, yanked her closer to him. She pulled her hand free, wrapped both arms over her stomach, as if to remove them from reach.

Simon lunged toward them, then reined himself in. What if he was wrong? What if she didn't need a champion? He looked back at his table.

His empty tankard. The perfect excuse.

After retrieving his cup, he quickly made his way to stand behind the chatty customer.

"Your father asked me to watch out for your interests, Remembrance, and that's what I'm doing. Trust me." The voice sounded familiar. Too familiar.

Graham Lott.

Simon seethed, his grip tightening on the pewter in his hand. He could stand up to the man's intimidation. He'd had years of practice. But could Mem?

"Once again you are putting conditions on your help." Her words were soft, but firm. "I don't believe Papa would have approved."

Simon lowered his head to hide a grin. Whatever the issue, Mem seemed to have it in hand. Simon had no right to interfere. He leaned back on his heels, ready to retreat. Until suddenly Mr. Lott was standing, his fingers wrapped around Mem's arm.

"I've been patient, Remembrance." His voice had turned menacing. "But I won't wait much longer. You need help. My help. And I will do whatever is required to convince you of that."

Enough.

"Excuse me." Simon stepped between them, forcing Lott to let go of Mem's arm. She immediately took a step backward. Simon put himself fully in the gap and held out his empty cup. "Could I trouble you for more ale?"

She blinked at him a couple of times, as if it took her a moment to comprehend his words. "Yes. Yes, of course." Snatching the tankard from his hand, she fled.

Simon retreated, his gaze on the floor. He had no desire to lay Mr. Lott's pride low. He did, after all, have a business arrangement with the scoundrel.

CHAPTER 7

SIMON RETURNED to his seat to find Timothy's wide-eyed gaze stuck to his face. Though all his muscles remained taut, he smiled at the lad, hoping to assure his son all was well. Men like Graham Lott didn't take well to being thwarted. But as Timothy returned to his storytelling, Simon began to relax.

Until the floor beneath his feet shook with the stomp of an angry man.

The entire room quieted as Simon raised his head to see Lott towering over him, the man's face dark as a thundercloud. Simon rose slowly, his eyes meeting Lott's on even ground. The dandy might have the advantage of weight, but in height they stood as equals.

"That was a private conversation." Lott ground out the words from between clenched teeth, as if he had no desire for everyone to know their business. "No one asked for your inter-ference."

"And I had no desire to interfere, sir, but for me parched throat."

Lott scraped his gaze over Simon, head to toe. "I might have known a dirty Irishman would need another drink."

41

Simon's fingers balled into his palm. *A dirty Irishman you didn't deign to take money from.* Uncurling his hand, he forced himself to shrug. He had no desire for a fight. Especially not in front of his son. But before he could return to his seat, Timothy flew to his feet and flung himself against Simon's leg, wrapping his arms around it and holding tight.

"Don't you talk to me Da that way!" He looked up at Simon then, and his face crumpled in confusion. "Don't let him talk that way, Da. Don't." Timothy was crying now, his tears dousing any desire in Simon to indulge his ire. He picked up his son, determined not to engage Lott in front of the lad. Lott held sway in this town, and while Rhode Island might not be Ireland, some things didn't change, no matter the country.

Timothy buried his head in Simon's shoulder. Simon stroked his son's head. "Hush now, lad. There'll be nothin' to cry for."

Murmurs rose in the silence, but whether in his defense or Lott's, Simon couldn't tell. One by one, attentions returned to food and drink. Simon sat down, holding Timothy on his lap, stroking his son's hair.

Lott leaned down, his breath heating Simon's ear. "I wouldn't rent to you should all my coffers be filled with dust."

Simon winced. "You'll be needin' this, then?" He fished the key from his pocket and held it out, snatching it back just as Lott made to grab it. "And me money? You'll be givin' that back when you get the key?"

Lott snorted, then stalked out the front door before Simon could speak another word, leaving his head swimming with the consequences of what he'd done. He rested his chin on Timothy's head. How would they survive now?

Before he could push back his chair and leave, Isaac Hyer set a small glass of spirits on the table in front of him. He looked up, met the man's sympathetic gaze.

Her nodded, an acknowledgment that he understood all that had transpired. "My compliments." he said. "Mem appreciated your help." Then he was off again, seeing to other patrons.

Simon hesitated only a moment before downing the drink. Then he threw a collection of coins on the table and carried Timothy out the door. They might as well sleep in the place they'd paid for, but he feared it would be a very expensive night.

How LONG HAD it been since she'd raced up the stairs and into Charity's parlor, putting her back to the door as if to blockade any entrant? She wasn't sure. But at least her breathing had slowed close to normal and her heart no longer seemed about to break through the confines of her chest.

Graham Lott be hanged! She should have guessed that his offer of help would be tied to her hand in marriage. Or rather, access to her property when she became his wife. Even if her apples had to rot on the trees and she lost everything, she wouldn't agree to marry the man. In fact, she might never acknowledge his existence again. She'd tried to be nice, for Papa's sake, but Papa wasn't here any more, and she doubted he'd approve his "friend's" methods of pursuing her.

Mem pushed away from the closed door, thankful Mr. Lott hadn't had the gall to follow her to the family rooms—and even more enamored of the man who'd made her escape possible. She'd read something intriguing in Simon Brennan's eyes when he'd held his empty cup toward her—almost an asking of permission to help. As if he didn't want to intrude should she have the situation in hand. As if anxious not to overstep the bounds of their new friendship.

Warmth oozed through her body like mulled wine on a wintery day. Then the glow vanished as quickly as if she'd locked herself in the ice house. Even if his physical appearance had caught her eye, even if his gallantry had ignited a sense of curiosity—even then she couldn't reveal any interest, no matter how benign. Not to Charity and Isaac. And certainly not to Simon himself, no matter the kind service he'd done her, whether by intent or not. But she could hold close the fact that the Lord had given her a champion against Mr. Lott's increasing advances just when she most needed it, even if that champion was for a moment instead of a lifetime.

"Charity?" she opened the door to the bedroom and poked her head inside.

"Shh." Charity put a finger to her lips as she knelt over the trundle bed occupied by all three little girls. Mem hurried across the room and helped her sister to her feet.

Charity grunted softly. "Thanks. It's not always easy to get up from that position these days."

"Why you are down on the floor in the first place is beyond me." Mem stooped to gently kiss each sleeping girl's forehead before steering her sister toward the parlor. Neither of them spoke until the door closed, barring their voices from the bedroom.

"I do it because they're my children, and they like it. We say our prayers before I tell them a story. I can't very well do that while towering above them." Charity eased down on the sofa, one hand splayed across the sphere of her stomach.

Remembrance dropped down beside her. "I know. I'm sorry." She clasped Charity's hand. "You are a good mother. But I worry—you know I worry—every time you are ready to birth another."

Charity pressed a kiss to the back of Mem's hand. "You and Isaac. If I'm at peace, why can't both of you be? The Lord has been my stay before, and He will be again." She shifted. "Now, Mem, what happened?"

Mem glanced away from Charity's piercing gaze. "Happened? Nothing happened."

"Of course something happened. Otherwise your face wouldn't be a lovely shade of rose, and you'd be down there, not up here. Did you break a piece of crockery? Or spill supper on a patron? Oh! Maybe you helped yourself to the spirits!" Charity giggled.

Mem huffed her reproof, let go of Charity's hand. "If you must know, Mr. Lott decided to add some 'conditions' to his earlier offer of help with my apples."

Charity snorted.

"Fine. You were right." Mem moved behind the rocking chair and set it in motion. "Which now leaves me in a bind. Unless by some miracle I can clear all the trees myself—and find someone to help get the apples to the ciderworks—I'll have little or no money to live on until next year's harvest." She rubbed circles on her temples, trying to quell the pounding in her head.

"At least you didn't give in and say yes."

Mem smirked. "There is that."

Quiet fell between them. A quiet which left Mem thinking of a dimpled smile beneath dark hair and eyes. Why had God left the embers of her age-old dream of a husband and family to smolder, to fan to life beneath a handsome face and a kind action? Why, when all she'd prayed since the day Solomon Hyer broke her heart was to be free from the desire to be loved by a man?

Mem crossed her arms and moved to the window, eager to feel the cool of the evening breeze. Sounds outside the Gray Goose drifted upward. Horses neighing. Dishes clanking. Voices ebbing and flowing like the tide. And framing the noise, the smell of salt from the sea.

"I wouldn't worry too much." Charity's loud yawn brought Mem around to face her once more.

"Go to bed, sister. You know the nights of sleep left to you are few."

Charity nodded as she lumbered to her feet. When reached the door to the bedroom, she turned back. "You'll return in the morning?"

"If Isaac needs me I will. But I have to check on things at the farm. For all I know, those urchins I shooed away last week have stripped the trees clean while I've been gone."

"But you'll be here for the baby, won't you?" Charity

suddenly looked eight years old again, asking Mem what they would do without a mother to care for them.

"The moment you send word, my foot will be on the road." Mem smiled then turned serious. "I'll be here, Charity. I promise."

OTHER THAN THE crackle of the fire before which Simon had spread their bedding, Timothy's even breathing was the only sound in the room. Thankfully, he'd unpacked nothing else of their meager belongings, so it wouldn't be difficult to leave tomorrow. At least, not to haul off their things. Definitely hard in other ways.

Fully clothed, Simon stretched out beside his son. He put his hands beneath his head and stared up at the flickering light on the ceiling. In the morning, he'd give Lott the key in exchange for his silver. Then he and Timothy would return to the Gray Goose, he supposed. He could find a boardinghouse, take his skill out to the countryside. He'd never thought of himself as an itinerant craftsman, but they needed income. Now. He had no idea how much of his coin would find its way back into his hand on the morrow. Less then he hoped, if he'd sized up Mr. Lott correctly. The law might offer him some hope of recovery, but justice never moved quickly enough for the one wronged.

Simon scowled. He'd been naive to imagine he could stomach even a business arrangement with such a lout. Ireland didn't hold all the odious men in the world. They lived scattered across the entire globe.

No matter. He needn't depend on such men to get forward in life. He had means of his own, thanks to Alannah. She might have brought her overbearing father into their marriage, but her frugality had made it possible for their family to escape him. Even if she hadn't survived to see it.

In the stillness, his mam's voice whispered from ages past.

Take no thought for the morrow: for the morrow shall take thought for the things of itself.

If only he could believe that were true. No tomorrow had yet brought Simon the relief he sought.

He turned over, determined to sleep, until a gentle knocking roused him again. His first thought was Lott, but if the man had come to make trouble now, he likely wouldn't be so timid. Simon hurried into the empty front room and glanced out the window, but he saw only night. The knock sounded again. He eased the door open.

Isaac Hyer stood in the shadows. "I have an idea."

CHAPTER 8

MEM HID upstairs with Charity until the customers drifted away and Isaac could drive her home. The entire ride she feared she would fall asleep on the wagon seat, tumble to the ground before reaching her bed. But once she stumbled into the house and the world quieted, Mem found herself wide awake. Hours later, she remained before the fire, the farmhouse parlor lit only by its flame.

Mr. Lott's lurking about, his insistence that she needed his help, left her frustrated and anxious and . . . raw. Shredded, as she had been all those years ago.

Her chin dropped to her chest, her neck as weak as a flower stem trying to support an apple. Even now she could conjure up Solomon Hyer's face in an instant. It wasn't hard, for every time she looked at Isaac she saw his older brother. The one who had wooed her, won her heart, then disappeared to marry a woman with a greater dowry.

"Why? Why? Why?" She shoved her fingers into her hair, raking them through until it spilled around her shoulders. Why did she still care?

Not for him. He'd killed her love long ago. But the rejection still stung. The betrayal. The unfaithfulness. She'd seen little reason not to assign such qualities to all men, except her father and Isaac. Graham Lott was no exception, especially since he hadn't given her a second glance until she inherited her father's fertile land. She'd learned in the months following Papa's death to recognize when male interest was sparked by her economic abundance. Those attentions didn't bother to look beyond her name, possibly her face. Certainly not to what resided inside her head and heart. The fact that Mr. Lott wanted her for what she possessed didn't feel any different than Solomon rejecting her for what she didn't. Neither showed the kind of love she expected from a spouse. The kind that Reverend Pilfer spoke of from the Scriptures.

She jumped to her feet in spite of her fatigue, paced around the room with new energy. She hadn't wavered in her quest for an independent life after Solomon left. She'd understood Papa wouldn't be around forever and that she'd either provide for herself or be forced to join the Hyer's household. Not that she didn't love Charity and Isaac and their children, but she didn't want to intrude. Or be a burden. She wanted to make a life of her own. On her own. That meant finding a way to get the crop in, proving to Mr. Lott—and everyone else—she could manage alone.

But even as she again firmed her resolve, unease brought her back to her chair, to the fireside. Mr. Lott hadn't been the only man to cross her path on a regular basis lately. There was also Mr. Brennan.

Simon. Her lips curled into a shy smile at the thought of his Christian name. His manner had drawn her in even before he'd come to her rescue. He'd talked of his son, his work. And though he'd said very little about the land or family he'd left behind, in his gaze she saw respect, which fanned her dormant hope to life once more. A man who offered help, but didn't make her feel weak. Whose attention didn't stem from obligation. And whose eyes seemed to say he admired her strength and her stand. Perhaps even her face and form.

Mem flushed hot. She told herself she sat too close to the fire and pushed her chair back a little. Then she clutched the cup of cold tea she'd long abandoned. Cold tea reminded her of Papa, of sitting near his bed while he lay dying. He'd spoken insistently to her, words about relying on God, not herself, about being open to change and help. Words reminding her of the Scripture that said two were better than one, and a strand of three cords was not quickly broken.

She'd nodded, squeezed his hand, and locked his sentiments in a box deep inside herself, unwilling to believe that even the God who ruled the universe could change her circumstances— or her heart.

Tears gathered in her eyes and slipped down her cheeks with each blink. Maybe Papa had been right. Even if Simon Brennan had no interest in her as a woman, maybe he'd been sent by God to pry open the heart she'd shut so tightly against hope. To give her the courage to ask for help, to admit she couldn't do everything alone. In truth, she hadn't even sought the help of God Almighty lately. Shaking her head, she reached for Papa's Bible and pulled it across the table. Turning to Genesis, she read the words into the silence. "In the beginning, God created the heaven and the earth."

As good a place to start as any.

THE SUN INCHED HIGHER as Simon carried their belongings to the Gray Goose, where he downed a cup of coffee, then hired a horse. He wouldn't leave Timothy behind. Not today. Mrs. Hyer didn't need one more rapscallion to look after, and Timothy might prove to be a help in his quest.

Setting Timothy on the saddle in front of him, Simon guided their mount out onto the north road. The morning's tangle with Lott had been a bitter one, leaving Simon with but a third of his money in his pocket. At least they weren't destitute. And wouldn't be, if Mem agreed to his plan.

Hyer's plan, actually. His appearance in the dark of night had been a godsend. The hope of an opportunity to work, a place to live. At least for the time being. He could continue to pursue a building for his shop, but with another source of income he might consider purchase instead of rent.

"Look, Da! Over there!" Timothy pointed to a stand of trees —leaves of gold and red and orange, with a bit of green interspersed between—beyond the path. "Did you see the bunny?" he squealed.

"A beauty of a land it is, son." Simon smiled, taking in the lush countryside and the glimpses of wildlife. No wonder The Gray Goose offered such rich fare. As his brother had written from his time in America during the war, it was, indeed, a land where all men could live like kings. Even if that meant turning his hand to a new trade, at least for a little while.

If only his heart didn't feel quite so heavy at the prospect.

He didn't mind asking a woman for a job, but why did it have to be this woman? The one whose very presence hammered away at the grief that guarded his heart? Of course, the news that she held land in her own right crushed even the hint of a hope of a possibility that there might ever be anything between them. He would not put himself in that position again, even if she didn't have a father to lord over him.

No, this would be an economic arrangement, pure and simple.

They continued on, meadow and forest giving way to fields. Finally, a stone house, a grove of trees spreading out behind. Just as Hyer described. Simon pulled the horse to a stop.

Timothy twisted to face him. "Are we here, Da?"

"We're here."

Timothy turned solemn. "Is it ours?"

Simon's throat tightened. No, not theirs. Hers. Mem's. She

stood high and above him, even higher than Alannah had, for Alannah's land and wealth had belonged to her father, not herself.

"Not ours, lad." He tousled the boy's hair before dismounting. "But we'll have somethin' like it one day. That we will. Some day, before you're a grown man. I promise you that."

Simon dismounted, then helped Timothy to the ground before tying the horse to a nearby post. Timothy slipped his hand into Simon's, as if sensing his da needed more courage than he owned.

Timothy. He was doing this for Timothy. For their future. With a sharp nod, he strode forward and rapped his knuckles hard on the door. Then he stepped back and waited.

And waited.

And waited.

"Maybe no one's at home." Timothy dashed toward the nearest window. Simon lunged for him, caught the fabric of his shirt, and held him back.

"I'll try again before we look around." Simon leaned forward, fist raised to rap again, but before his knuckles met wood, the door swung open. Mem stood before him, wheat-colored hair disheveled, clothing winkled, her wide mouth forming a perfect O. Simon swiped his hat from his head as Timothy launched himself at the lady, arms tight around her legs, cheeks pressed into her skirt. A trill of laughter followed the spark in her eyes.

She cupped Timothy's chin and lifted it toward hers. "What are you doing here, little man?"

Then her face went white as she jerked her gaze to Simon. "Charity?"

"No, no. Nothin' like that." Simon cleared his throat, unable to keep his eyes on hers. "We came because Mr. Hyer said you might be in need of some labor—and I am currently in need of some work."

"Work, Mr. Brennan?" Color rose into her cheeks, adding to her allure. "I thought you had a shoe shop to open in town."

Simon squinted into the fields to his right, suddenly wary of what had seemed a good plan. How to explain without making her feel at fault, making her feel as if she had no choice but to take him on? He mashed his lips into a frown. This was a bad idea. In every way.

"I'm sorry to have troubled you." After a quick bow, he slapped his hat on his head, clasped Timothy's hand, and turned to leave.

"I want to stay!"

Simon whipped around to face the lad, embarrassment fanning the flames of anger.

Timothy grabbed the doorframe and held on. "I. Want. To. Stay!"

Simon stood back, blew out a breath of frustration. Until he heard a chocked giggle. A cough. Another muffled giggle. He fought a grin rising of its own accord. He couldn't blame the lad. He wanted to stay here, too.

He glanced at Mem, who had taken to chewing her bottom lip as she studied him. She was considering. That much was clear. Best wait out her decision before doing anything rash.

"If Isaac sent you . . ." The concern in her eyes nearly unraveled him. "I'm just . . . confused. But please—" she laid a hand on his arm "stay. I'd be grateful for the help."

"Please, Da?" Timothy looked up at Simon with Alannah's eyes. Suddenly it was if she were pleading for her son's life—the life of freedom they'd dreamed. Even if it happened without her. He had never refused anything his wife had asked of him. How could he now refuse her son?

CHAPTER 9

MEM WALKED TOWARD THE ORCHARD, hearing Simon and Timothy following behind. What on earth had Isaac been thinking, sending them to her? And yet she guessed it made sense. At least to Isaac. For how could he know the thoughts that had been swirling in her head over this man?

She stopped beneath a tree near the back of the grove, picked up a basket and handed it to Simon, her hand brushing his, her face warming as it would beneath the midday sun.

He looked up the ladder set against the tree, then pushed the basket back toward Mem. "Do you have a second ladder, perchance?"

"In the barn." She nodded toward the wooden structure.

"Right, then." He clapped a hand to Timothy's shoulder. "Come along, lad. We'll bring it 'round." Then he looked at Mem, his expression serious. "With the two of us climbin' and pickin', we'll have this crop in before the snow flies."

Mem watched them go, watched Simon's head tip toward his son in conversation, saw the boy laugh, then smile at his father, take his hand. It put her in mind of Isaac with his girls, their easy banter, their unrestrained laughter. Isaac was a good father. A good husband. A good man. Might Simon Brennan be cut from similar cloth?

Stop it. The man had come to help her bring in her apples. Nothing more. And the quicker they accomplished that task, the better. She grabbed her bag and climbed up into the tree once more, her fingers working as fast as they could.

Grab, twist, pull, drop. Grab, twist, pull, drop.

"Da! I brought the water!" Timothy grunted to raise the half-full bucket. Simon lifted it to his lips and drank deeply before swiping his arm first across his mouth, then his sweaty forehead. Setting his hand on his hips, he stared into the sky. A few more hours of daylight, and he intended to use them all.

"Auntie Mem, do you want some?" Timothy clung to the ladder as she descended. Simon reached them in two large steps, took the heavy bag of apples from her, and gently transferred them to a bushel basket nearby. Timothy grabbed her hand and dragged her to the water bucket. He peered inside, then looked up at her in consternation. "I'll go get more."

Before Simon or Mem could reply, Timothy had picked up the bucket, his little legs churning back toward the stone well house.

"He certainly has a lot of energy." Mem kept her eyes on the lad as she spoke.

"Indeed he does. At least when he's wantin' to please."

Silence fell between them then. An awkward silence. One that left Simon searching for something to say. He cleared his throat, looked out across the orchard.

"We'll have made good progress by sundown."

"Yes, I expect so." Her hands worried in front of her, and he wondered what about him set her so on edge, especially after they'd settled into such an easy friendship at the Gray Goose. Was she nervous to be on her own with him, or did her mind continue to hearken back to Lott's threats? He'd thought perhaps his presence would dispel her fear, not feed it.

"Mem—"

Her head turned sharply. His gaze found the ground.

"I want you to know how much we appreciate the work. And the lodging. I looked over the barn earlier. It will suit us fine." He hoped his words would bring relief to her face. Instead, she seemed confused.

"I'm back!" Timothy plopped the bucket at Mem's feet, cool water splashing over the rim, dousing Mem's skirt and shoes. She picked up the bucket and drank, the excess spilling down her chin, soaking her bodice. Now she matched Timothy, who seemed to have gathered more water on his clothing than in the bucket.

Simon rubbed his chin to hide a smile. He loved that his son wanted to help, but perhaps he loved even more that Mem let him, in spite of the mess he created.

"Will you help me move my ladder to the next tree?" Mem said to Timothy.

Timothy nodded, bounded forward. They walked away, their chatter both warming and alarming Simon. How could he not feel drawn to a woman who appreciated his child? And yet as he let himself take in the large grove of trees, the acres of farmland, he knew he could not indulge in any inclination toward her. At least nothing of more than a friendly nature. For he refused to join himself again to a woman with means above his own.

CHAPTER 10

MEM WINCED as she rolled over and sat up in the box bed that had belonged to her parents. Every part of her body ached. All the climbing, stretching, and carrying of the day before had taken their toll. But oh, how thankful she was to have Simon's assistance. Her lips twitched into a small smile. And Timothy's. They were not only helping her empty her trees, they'd brought such joy to the process. Companionship she'd thought couldn't be replaced after Papa died.

Her smile widened as she hugged her knees while picturing the barrels the cooper had delivered lined up along the back wall of the house. No need to carry them to the cellar. Another week or two and they'd have the trees picked clean. Some she'd keep, for herself and the Gray Goose. But for the majority of her crop, she'd hire a wagon and she and Simon—and Timothy—would drive the rest to the ciderworks or ship captains.

She flexed arms and legs, fingers and feet, and thanked God for sending the Brennans. For truly they were a gift—both of them. They were grateful for the work; she was grateful for the assistance. Just one more reason why she ought not worry over Graham Lott—or anything else for that matter. Just as Papa had said, her Father God, who cared for the lowliest of sparrows, knew exactly what she'd needed. And when.

If only He hadn't sent that that help wrapped in such fine packaging, both inside and out.

She pushed to her feet and hobbled about the room, not bothering to poke up the embers in the grate. Clothed in an old dress and boots, she stole down the stairs to stir the kitchen fire into flame. But to her surprise, Simon bent over the hearth, the orange and yellow light illuminating his pensive face. An unidentifiable joy rose within her. But then she paused, her smile fading. Why was he in the house? When had he come? She hadn't heard him arrive.

She didn't think him capable of harm, but he'd come in without permission. Had she allowed too many intimacies already? Yet even as fear fluttered in her chest, she realized he hadn't stepped beyond the kitchen. Then a new thought struck. He didn't mean to leave yet, did he? Suddenly she found herself more afraid of his absence than his unexpected presence.

No sense in speculation. She might as well know the worst.

She let her foot land on the stone floor, catching his attention. "Good morning, Mr. Brennan." She moved past him to tend the kettle already steaming over the flame. "Tea? The water appears near to boiling."

"Yes, but you needn't serve me, Miss Wilkins. I know my way around a teapot." His smirk set her stomach tumbling, her cheeks heating. She stepped back from the fire, her gaze skittering to the back door. To escape.

She swallowed hard. "I'll get the milk from the spring house, then," she whispered before heading outside. With the door closed behind her, she breathed a bit of relief.

She didn't quite know how to respond to such attentiveness. Such kindness. He unsettled her now as he had yesterday in the orchard, managing to be both industrious hired help and doting father, stirring her heart more than she cared to admit.

Mem scolded herself as she trudged ahead on her errand.

His manner oughtn't matter. Her interest in him lay only in the service he could provide, his in the employment she offered. Her heart had no place in the situation at all.

LATER THAT AFTERNOON, Simon climbed into the top of a tree to reach for the highest apples. From this vantage point he could see the progress they'd made. Several trees picked clean, though with many yet to go.

The physical labor felt better than he'd expected, even beyond the feeling that his hours had a worthwhile aim. The bag at his side strained with the load as he searched through the leaves for any remaining fruit before heading down the ladder. He reached the ground at the same time as Mem did from the tree in front of him, her bag bulging just slightly less than his.

Timothy jumped up from beneath a different tree and ran to help them stack the apples in the baskets that Simon would soon carry to the barrels next to the house. Simon cut his eyes towards Mem, admiring both her grace and strength to work alongside him. Or maybe he worked alongside her.

Didn't matter. He enjoyed it, even if they didn't have much conversation, each of them up in a different tree. Still, he watched her. She laughed at Timothy, smiled at the progress of filled baskets. But then a wrinkle appeared along her forehead.

He stepped nearer, kept his voice low. "What's botherin' you, lass?"

The winkles deepened. "Bothering?"

"Aye. You look . . . worried."

"I am. About Charity." She glanced at Timothy before responded further. "A babe is a beautiful gift, but always a danger."

"'Tis indeed. At least for some. But she's healthy and strong."

"Yes, but they—well, we never have much time." Her face

pinked, as if she suddenly realized the focus of their conversation. Childbirth wasn't a subject meant for a man and woman of such small acquaintance. She turned and scampered up the ladder. To hide her embarrassment, he guessed.

Simon dusted off his hands, wishing he could assure her all would be well. But he couldn't. Some things weren't certain. And as she said, children were a gift but also a danger. Best to return to work, as she had. But first he sought the water bucket, now supplied with a dipper. After drenching his insides, he doused his outside. The water soaked into his hair, dripped down his face, to his shoulders, neck, and chest. A vigorous shake of his head sent excess droplets arcing through the dappled sunshine and onto the carpet of grass at his feet.

And produced a high-pitched squeal.

He stilled, turned.

Mem's back was too him, hunched, as if to protect herself from the spray.

When had she climbed back down? He swallowed hard, fear settling like a stone in his middle. Would she be as indulgent toward him as she was toward his son?

"I'm so sorry. I should have—"

She faced him now, eyes wide, mouth twitching. "No need to apologize, Mr. Brennan." She smoothed her droplet-dotted dress. "I confess, I never knew the presence of a bit of water on one's person could feel so . . . satisfying."

Simon toed the grass, wondering if she would be offended by his grin. And then her skirt came into his downturned view. He looked up, slowly. Caught the glimmer of humor in her eyes.

"Mightn't you—I mean . . ." She turned her face away from him, as if she couldn't bear to say the words and see his face at the same time. "No need to hurry away after supper tonight. I would enjoy the company of an evening." She managed to look at him now. "You and Timothy."

Simon put a hand to his chest and bowed slightly. "We'd be honored . . . Mem."

When he looked up, she'd disappeared into the treetop again. Yes, he could use the company of an evening as well, the conversation of another adult. He only wished the anticipation of an evening with this particular person didn't come with quite such a burst of joy.

AFTER SUPPER, with the three of them settled in front of the fire, Simon's hands returned to the familiar work of fashioning a pair of shoes, this time for his son. Mem pulled a book from a shelf on the wall.

"Do you like stories, Timothy?"

He nodded, climbed into her lap at her invitation. She opened the book. "Chapter 1. I was born in the year 1632, in the city of York, of a good family, though not of that country, my father being a foreigner of Bremn, who settled first at Hull."

Simon smiled as he worked, recognizing the familiar lines from *Robinson Crusoe* and enjoying the quiet cadence of Mem's voice. Two chapters in, Timothy slid from her lap and curled in front of the warm fire like a contented cat. Within moment, he was purring in slumber.

Mem's voice slowed, than stopped. "I don't want him to miss anything. It's a very exciting story."

"Aye. One of my favorites." Simon quit his own work, began gathering his supplies. "I ought to put him in bed. Myself, too. Another long day tomorrow." He smiled, hoping she could read his gratitude at such a familial evening, too reticent to put his feelings into words.

She started to rise from her chair, then returned to it. "You needn't take your things away, Mr. Brennan."

"Simon. Please call me Simon."

A hesitant nod. "Simon. You may leave your things here. They won't be in the way, and then you needn't take the time to set up your work again tomorrow evening."

"Thank you, Mem" He scooped up his son, carried him to

the door. Mem met him there, pulled it open for him.

He nodded as he stepped into the chill night air. "Until tomorrow," he said.

"Tomorrow," she whispered in reply.

The faint square of light spilling into the yard remained visible until he pulled the barn doors shut behind them.

ANOTHER COMPANIONABLE MORNING in the kitchen, then out among the trees. His bag filled quickly with apples, his hands accustomed, now, to his task, leaving his mind free to roam. He glanced around, wondering where Mem was working, but he didn't spy her. For the best, he told himself as he attended to his task once again. For the more conversation they'd managed, the more his admiration for her grew. Grew to the point that he found himself both dreading and welcoming the end of their acquaintance. Once he had money in hand again, he intended to seek a place to ply his trade, preferably a place away from the likes of Mr. Lott.

But the thought didn't satisfy as much as it once had. Not with Timothy to consider. The lad rarely left Mem's side, calling her Auntie Mem as the Hyer children did. And Mem didn't make it easy to leave her out of the equation, either, for she responded in kind, treating his son as one would expect of a doting aunt.

Or a loving mother.

Simon's chest constricted. Whether he stayed in Providence or escaped to another town in this vast land, there would be pain. Best not think about that yet. Decisions could be made once the crop was in.

He climbed down the ladder with a full bag at his hip just in time to see Mem and Timothy, hands clasped, working their way toward the house. Gently, he emptied his bag into a bushel-basket, heaved the basket into his arms, and strode toward empty barrels waiting to be filled.

CHAPTER 11

THREE DAYS LATER, with his head among the leafy branches, Simon listened for Mem and Timothy, his ear tuned to hear their chattering or laughter. Yet only grasses and leaves sang in the light breeze. He climbed down, but couldn't see them, either. Perhaps they'd gone to the well for a drink of water. Or to the house for a bite to eat. But that wasn't like Mem. She'd worked these past days just as hard as he had. And as long. And always with Timothy scampering about nearby.

He hefted a full basket of apples and carried it to the barrels waiting besides the house, still pondering the whereabouts of the orchard owner and his son. Voices carried on a sudden gust of wind. Nearby, but still out of sight.

"I told you, I have it in hand." Mem, her words hard and unyielding.

"You're gathering all the fruit? From every tree? Hauling it to the ciderworks? Bartering for your price? And you think they'll take you seriously?" Lott's gravelly voice grated across Simon's nerves. Taking long strides, he rounded the corner of the house.

"If you must know, I have help." Mem rested her arm across Timothy's shoulders, as if a four-year-old were any help at all.

Simon forced himself to walk, not run. To stop beside Mem instead of ramming his shoulder into Lott's gut and taking him to the ground.

Lott scowled. "Him?"

"Yes." Mem glanced at Simon, her eyes clouded in confusion. As if she didn't understand the ill will between the men. But then, she didn't. Not completely. And he had no desire to rectify her ignorance of the matter.

"You realize he's Irish. Likely a papist," Lott spat.

Mem turned a haughty face to the man. "And we in Rhode Island have always been most tolerant of those who worship differently than we do, Mr. Lott."

Simon's mouth dropped open, her defense of him further seeding his admiration.

Lott grunted, eyes trained on Mem. "He's like to steal you blind."

Her chin lifted just a touch. "He's been only kind and attentive." Another glance at Simon, her expression softening. "A gentleman in every respect. Besides, he has a trade of his own. He just needs time to secure the right situation."

Simon looked away from the admiration clearly visible in her eyes, a lump in his throat making it hard to swallow. Blimey, but the lady made it hard for him to hold on to his heart.

"Don't be taken in," Lott continued. "He wants your land, not you. He's toying with your affections. Making himself indispensable. I'd even venture to say that his 'skill' at shoe making is more ruse than reality."

Simon longed to smash his fist into the lying buffoon's mouth. But he would not defend himself, not if it meant letting loose the truth of their connection. Or rather the reason for its dissolution. He didn't want Mem to carry that burden.

"Come, Me—Miss Wilkins," Simon extended his crooked arm. "We still have work to do."

Her attention remained on Lott. "Why would you accuse him of such a thing? What has he ever done to you?"

Disquiet stirred Simon's belly. He had to forestall this conversation. He reached for Mem's hand, placed it on his arm, and tried to walk away, to pull Mem and Timothy, who now clung to her hand, with him. But she refused to move. Stiff as a marble statue, she waited for Lott's response.

The odious man stepped closer, his nose almost touching Mem's. "Why else would I have flung him out of my building unless I'd discovered something of his nefarious ways?"

Simon barreled toward the man, slammed him to the earth and smacked a fist into his face. Again. And again. And again. It felt good, the physical release of his pent up anger. Too good. He barely noticed Mem and Timothy screaming until he felt them pulling at him with their hands, Lott cackling at him between punches. Finally, finally, reason overcame his rage. He sat back, breathing hard. Lott's eye was purpling, his nose spewing blood. As the man scrambled up from the ground, his smirk made Simon want to return to the beating. Only Timothy's wide-eyed silence held him in check.

"*That* is your 'gentleman'?" Lott dabbed at his nose with a square of linen he'd drawn out of the pocket of his coat. "My offer of help stands, Remembrance. But only if you order this man off your property today. After that, I am no longer responsible for what happens."

Mem stalked toward Lott, her finger poised as if to jab into his chest. "You've never been responsible for what happens to me, Mr. Lott. I'm perfectly capable of taking care of myself." Her hand dropped to her skirt. She curtseyed. "I bid you good day, sir." Whirling around, she grabbed Simon's arm and dragged him toward the orchard, Timothy running alongside, looking back every few steps until the sound of Lott's galloping horse faded away.

Then Mem slowed. Sheltered by the house now, she let go of his arm and leaned into the cool, stone walls, looking as if she might faint. He slipped an arm around her shoulders, brought his lips near her ear. "Let me take you inside. To rest."

She stiffened beneath his touch, then closed her eyes and shook her head, her lips trembling.

"I'm fine, Mr--Simon." She opened her eyes again, let her gaze roam his face. Her fingertips grazed the spot near his eye where Lott had managed to strike. He winced, wishing he hadn't risen to the man's bait. "But you——" She smiled, but with a new sadness. A fresh uncertainty. "We have work to do, have we not? Come, Timothy." She held out her hand to the lad. "Let's choose another tree to empty."

As she walked ahead of him, hand in hand with his son, Simon sensed a loss of something between them, but whether from Lott's accusations or Simon's own actions, he couldn't tell.

Either way, it might be best if he and Timothy took their leave now, before their hearts became too entangled. For as much as he enjoyed Mem's company, he couldn't foresee a future together. Especially now. For if she hadn't considered before that he had nothing and she had everything, Lott's insinuations would likely cause her to question Simon's motives in every regard.

Yes, he would cut ties. Move southward, down the coast. Seek another new beginning. After all, he had nothing to keep him in Providence, Rhode Island. Especially not Miss Remembrance Wilkins.

CHAPTER 12

MEM STEPPED INTO A COLD, quiet kitchen the next morning. Her heart seemed to jump into her throat and stick there, making it hard to swallow. It had been disconcerting though somewhat wonderful to wake each of the past few days to a crackling fire in the kitchen, Simon's dimpled grin greeting her as he poured her tea. Even though he always left Timothy asleep in their makeshift room in the barn, they would converse in quiet morning tones, as if afraid to wake the sleeping child. When Timothy wandered in, they tended to bustle about the room, a bit shy of one another. Not that Timothy seemed to notice.

In fact, though she didn't care to admit it completely, the mornings and evenings with Simon and Timothy had been a soothing balm to her lonely heart. Almost as if they were . . . a family.

Until the fisticuffs yesterday shattered that perfect world. Still, they'd returned to work, albeit quieter. And spent last evening reading and working in front of the fire after supper, as had become their habit.

So she hadn't expected a cold and empty kitchen to greet her this morning.

Forcing herself to the normal morning tasks, she poked up the banked fire before peeking out the back door for some sign of Simon. Had he gone away? Assumed for some reason she wouldn't want him to stay? Movement among the trees caught her eye. Her body tensed, ready to give chase to a juvenile intruder. Until her vision clarified.

Simon, not the little thieves from before.

So he hadn't gone. But he hadn't come into the kitchen for their comfortable chat, either. She eased the door shut, kept her hands busy with a light meal to fortify them for the day of harvest ahead. Her mind wandered as she worked, jumping back to Graham Lott's words the previous afternoon.

He's toying with your affections. Making himself indispensable. Don't be taken in. He wants your land, not you.

She'd tried to set the accusation aside, see it for what it was —an attempt to put forward a case for himself. But it was hard to ignore the possibility of truth. Simon Brennan owned nothing. And though she had seen evidence of his cobbling skill, he could have realized the prosperity of her farm and decided to try his hand at her instead of at shoemaking. She couldn't say for certain. She'd known the man less than a fortnight.

She shook her head. What had she been thinking?

She hadn't. That was the answer. Now she must steel her heart against him or she'd find herself bereft of the independence she cherished. Another week and the crop would be in and sold. She couldn't toss Simon and Timothy out before she'd fulfilled her end of the bargain. But she could hurry the harvesting process, the time he remained in her employ.

In the meantime, she'd keep her distance from Simon. As for Timothy, she'd treat him as she did her nieces. Attached, but not unnaturally so.

The door opened. Timothy sprinted inside and attached himself to Mem in a tight hug. Simon followed more slowly.

"Mr. Brennan." She nodded a polite greeting then set the meal on the table. They ate, Timothy's words filling the silence between them.

THE HUSH CONTINUED as they worked in the orchard. And Simon hated it. Hated the loss of pleasant conversation and hated that he noticed it. Hated the damage of Lott's words about his character and hated that he couldn't tell Mem the truth of the situation. Well, not couldn't. Wouldn't. If he told her she was the reason Lott had tossed him out, he'd never know if her affections had found purchase in her heart or her conscience.

Not that he could entertain any such feelings himself. Not with the disparity of their financial situations. He would not be beholden to a woman again. But he wished for their former ease of conversation, even if it had no other aim than companionship.

He climbed down the ladder, stretched this arms in the air. His muscles weren't accustomed to this type of labor. Nor to the physicality of his . . . conversation with Lott yesterday. A grin teased his mouth. Sending the man to the ground had made him feel better. For the moment.

Mem strode past him. He reached out but let his arm fall without touching her. "Mem—Miss Wilkins."

"Yes?" She looked up at him with a mixture of wariness and delight. As if she couldn't decide if he were friend or foe.

"I, uh," he stuck his hands in his pockets and looked away, missing the natural ease that had been between them. He scratched in the dirt with the toe of his boot. "I'm sorry for yesterday, for fightin'. A fool of a thing to do, I ken." He jerked his head up, anxious for her response.

Her tight-lipped smile didn't set him at ease.

He swallowed hard. "I embarrassed you."

"As did he, Mr. Brennan. Boys Timothy's age know how to act better then the two of you." She set her hands on her slim hips. "Can you at least explain why he denied you use of his building?"

Simon's jaw tightened. He stared off into the distance. He wouldn't lie, but he wouldn't acknowledge her part in the situation. "We realized a fundamental disagreement is all. It wouldna have worked for either of us, in the end."

"And that would be because . . . ?" Her gaze pierced through him, sharp as a sword. Surely she wouldn't turn on him so quickly, not after he'd proven himself helpful these past few days.

But then, he'd done exactly what Lott had said. Made himself indispensable. Yes, she likely believed every word. Or had come to, after a night's musings. After all, she'd known Lott far longer than Simon, and him only Irish.

Timothy ran between them, a lizard skating up his arm as he laughed. Mem shifted, crossed her arms before allowing them to drop to her sides. As if she were giving up some fight he wasn't privy to.

"I need to go into town and check on Charity. I'm worried about her."

He nodded, began the journey toward the house with a basket of apples. She walked beside him, matching his stride, Timothy gamboling about them like a colt in spring.

"And I think while I'm there I'll hire some more help." She raised her face to the sky. "Might storm. I can't afford any more delay."

Simon could only nod, his chest rumbling with the betrayal. She wanted him gone. Soon. That much was clear. Yet as much as he hated the thought of her mistrust, perhaps this was for the best. With other workers coming, he wouldn't feel obliged to stay. And suddenly he had a fierce desire to move on.

CHAPTER 13

As MEM REACHED the edge of town, the rain started. Slow, fat drops at first. Then they came more quickly, stinging her skin and soaking her clothes. She pulled the cloth more securely over the basket of newly picked apples for the Hyers.

By the time she reached the Gray Goose, her skirt and petticoats felt heavy as iron, her feet slippery as eels. Every eye in the dining room turned as she breached the door. Mem gritted her teeth, determined not to cry—until she realized her tears would be indistinguishable from the water sluicing down her face. And so she allowed them to flow, hot tears mingling with cold rain. She started to shiver, body shaking, teeth chattering. Then Isaac was next to her, throwing a blanket around her, taking the basket of fruit from her hand.

"What's wrong? I told you I could handle the dining room." He led her toward the stairs.

"I know. I just needed to check on Charity." Her mouth quivered. She couldn't reveal her foolishness over Simon Brennan. Not to Isaac. He'd feel it so deeply, another close connection to her broken heart. First his brother then the man he'd sent to work for her.

"Don't worry over me. I'm perfectly capable of taking care of myself." Mem patted Isaac's cheek before mounting the stairs. She just wanted to be warm and dry. To sip a hot cup of cider or tea. Even coffee would do. To have Charity fuss over her as if she were one of the little girls.

After a swift knock, she pushed open the door to the family's rooms.

"Charity?" The parlor was askew—and empty. Mem lifted her skirt, trying not to drag mud across the rug on her way to the bedroom. "Charity?"

"Auntie Mem!" Grace raced from her mother's bedside and into Mem's wet skirt. Mem held the child away from her as the other girls followed, imagining Charity's pursed lips turning to a frown at the thought of more laundry to do. But she didn't see her sister. Not at first glance.

Then she noticed the writhing beneath the bedsheets, the low moan accompanying the movement. "Charity?"

Without thought of her wet clothing, Mem sat on the edge of the feather ticking. A sheen of sweat covered Charity's gray face, her eyes cinched shut, teeth clutching her bottom lip.

"Grace," Mem kept her voice calm. "Go get your papa. Now."

The patter of tiny feet told her the girl had obeyed. Mem found a cloth and dipped it in the nearby basin of water, then she wiped Charity's forehead, spoke her sister's name once more.

Charity's eyes fluttered open. She clutched at Mem's muddy gown. "Help me."

Mem's mouth went dry. She leapt to her feet and rushed from the room. She met Isaac on the stairs.

"I'm going for Mrs. Gladstone." Before she could continue her descent, two strong hands on her arms stopped her progress.

"You stay," Isaac said. "I'll go."

He darted down again, leaving her to on unsteady legs for a

moment before she could force her steps upward once more, praying as she went.

~

"BUT WHERE ARE WE GOING, DA?" Timothy clenched his fingers more tightly around Simon's hand, his little legs churning to keep up with Simon's long stride.

"I told you. We're getting on a ship."

"Again?" He wrinkled his nose, tried to tug Simon to a stop. "But I wanna stay with Auntie Mem. I like it here." His bottom lip poked out in a pout. Simon would've thrown the lad over his shoulder and carried him away, but their meager belongings already hung about him, weighing him down. He glanced into the sky. The rain had abated. He prayed it wouldn't commence again until they reached town. The thought of slogging through mud with all their things and Timothy nearly sent him running back to Mem's barn and orchard.

Nearly.

But in truth, he had no choice. Whether she'd realized it or not, she'd given him the means to go by declaring her intention to bring back more laborers. It was what she wanted. What *he* wanted. Wasn't it?

He thought again about telling her the truth of Lott's accusation. Would he, if she were a man? Or if she had no tug on his heart?

Perhaps.

Which bothered him even more. No lass who had tried to catch his eye since Alannah succumbed to the fever had succeeded. Now this one—this woman endowed with land of her own—hadn't tried to sway his heart but had captured it all the same.

And there lay the difficulty. His heart *was* involved. Timothy's, too. He glanced down at his son tripping along beside him, hiccuping with unspent sobs, tears tracking down his cheeks. Simon groaned, imagining Alannah tutting at him, putting a hand to his cheek and telling him to take more care for himself and the lad.

He shook away the vision, but slowed his pace. No matter his complicated feelings, he still couldn't reconcile himself to being in Mem's debt. So though it would hurt them both to leave this place, leave they must.

They fell into a silent rhythm, reached town as the heavens opened again. Simon dashed into the first shipping office they came too, found passage on a morning packet to New York, then settled them at the Blue Mermaid, a rowdy inn near the wharf with passable fare and dirty rooms. But at least Mem wasn't there. Nor any memories of her. And come morning, they'd be gone.

RAINDROPS SPLATTERED against the glass windows, obscuring the view into the darkening day.

"Auntie Mem, we're scared," Grace lisped, standing in the doorway with Agnes, their hands clasped tightly to each other's.

Mem glanced at Charity, then led her nieces back into the parlor, where Clara fussed at being abandoned. "Play pat-a-cake with your sister until I get back." She laid her hand gently on each child's head before moving back toward the bedroom door.

"Auntie Mem," Agnes whimpered. "Don't leave."

Clara let out a wail. Mem squeezed her eyes shut and prayed for patience. And for Charity. Then she looked down at her nieces, determined to appear as unruffled as they needed her to be.

"I need to look in on your mama. Papa will be up soon with your supper."

The two older girls nodded. Aggie sat on the floor and pulled Clara into her lap while Grace started to sing. Mem dashed back to her sister's room.

Charity was quieter now, though sweat trickled down her face in the same way the rain slicked down the windows. The bedclothes were damp and limp. Mem reached for a cloth, dipped it in the tepid water in the bowl beside the bed and dabbed her sister's face. A faint smile rewarded her.

"Hold on, dear. Mrs. Gladstone must be on her way by now."

A slight nod, then a tight jaw and closed eyes, the arch of her back in pain. All without uttering a sound.

Mem sat on the edge of the bed and lifted her sister's hand. Charity's grip tightened as the wind whistled through the small alley between buildings. A storm was certainly brewing outside. She listened for a sound on the stairs.

Nothing. Where was Isaac?

Charity eased. Mem used the opportunity to wander to the window overlooking the street. She needed Mrs. Gladstone. Or at the very least, Isaac. The two of them had birthed Clara together. They could do it again, if need be. Pressing her nose against the glass, Mem searched the watery haze that was the street for some sign of him. As she did, her mind wandered to the farm. She hoped Simon had thought to cover the apple barrels and protect what they'd already harvested.

Footsteps pounded up the stairs. Mem turned as Isaac burst into the room.

"How is she?" He spoke to Mem, but his gaze stayed fixed on Charity. The love shining from his eyes left Mem's heart in a puddle. In the beginning she'd feared he'd be as unfaithful as his brother. But he'd proven his integrity in these past few years. Truly, if she couldn't be the recipient of such a steadfast love herself, she was glad it belonged to Charity.

"We're managing." She glanced past Isaac, raised her eyebrows when his gaze finally met hers. He gave a slight shake of his head.

So no help. Fine. They could do this. Mem pulled her shoulders back in determination—just as Charity's face contorted with pain.

Everything else faded away then. The noise of the girls and Isaac in the room next door. The lashing of wind around the eaves of the building. The patter of rain upon the roof. For this moment, nothing existed beyond Charity and her babe and their fight for life.

For a small person, Charity could grip with amazing strength. Mem anchored her feet to the floor to bear it. She refused to cry out. Refused to flinch. Refused to even move, other than to lean closer, to whisper words of encouragement as her sister's eyes cinched shut and her teeth ground into one another. Mem prayed for the strength of God to sustain them, then called for Isaac and readied herself to receive Charity's child.

THE BABE CAME QUICKLY, once it decided to come. As it slid into Mem's hands, Mrs. Gladstone burst through the door and shed her oilcloth cloak, flinging water to the corners of the room.

Mem gazed down at the small, bloody body, its mouth open in screaming protest of the cold, new world. "It's a boy!" Her heart swelled with love for her nephew, even as it pinched with the thought that she'd never know a child of her own.

Mrs. Gladstone rolled up her sleeves and bustled in to take over. Mem held the child while Mrs. Gladstone cut the cord, then Mem handed the boy to Isaac to wrap in a clean swathe of flannel. Mem would bathe the baby in a little while, after Charity met her son and rested from her labor.

"Another fine child, Mrs. Hyer." Mrs. Gladstone talked as she worked. "And my guess is he'll rule the roost with his sisters." She laughed, her large chest shaking with joviality.

Isaac kissed his son's head before handing him down to Charity. "Indeed he will."

The room settled into silence. Mrs. Gladstone cleaned Charity and readied her for sleep while Mem washed her nephew's fresh skin. When Charity's breathing evened, Isaac tiptoed from the room to get some rest on the parlor sofa. His day would begin again before first light.

The window glass rattled in a gusty swirl of wind, raindrops slapping in the aftermath. Mem thought of her apples, prayed the ones still on the trees would remain there for now. And that Simon and Timothy would be safe and dry.

The midwife's mouth stretched into a large yawn.

"Go on home, Mrs. Gladstone. I can watch over Charity and the baby."

Mrs. Gladstone nodded. "I think I will, if you don't mind." She glanced at the window, the patter of rain having grown suddenly faint. "Perhaps I'll make it home before another deluge." She secured her oilcloth cloak, then her bonnet. "Been out three nights straight. I'd like a few hours warm and dry in my own bed."

Before she left, the midwife brushed her fingers over the baby's forehead and smiled. "It never gets old," she whispered. Then she was gone, leaving Mem in the peaceful silence of mother and babe.

CHAPTER 14

SIMON SHOOK his son's shoulder before the hands of his pocket watch stretched between twelve and six. "Time to get up, lad."

Timothy sat up, rubbed his eyes. "The ship, Da?"

"The ship." Simon tousled Timothy's already unruly hair.

It didn't take long for them to gather their things, eat a quick bowl of soupy porridge. When they stepped outside the shelter of the Blue Mermaid into a moderate rainfall, Timothy glanced up at Simon, his eyes questioning.

"Ships continue t' sail when it's rainin'." Though he didn't remind that it made for a more rollicking ride. He hoped neither the lad nor himself would spend the trip with head hanging over a bucket.

No help for that now. Their passage was booked. They were expected. They had to go.

Simon hurried them to the quay, boarded a skiff. Two brawny sailors rowed them out to the *Harriet May*.

Simon's chin tipped toward the sky as the small boat bobbed in the water. The rain had slackened a bit, but the wind seemed on the increase. A rope ladder hanging over the side of the packet twisted with each new gust, landing with a slap against the side of the vessel.

Simon set Timothy's feet on the first rung and directed his hands to the side ropes. Timothy shook his head and turned back to cling to his father. "I can't, Da," he cried into Simon's shoulder.

The two sailors in the skiff were getting restless. Simon shushed the lad's weeping and pulled him close.

"Take the boy on your back and haul him aboard," one grumbled. The other nodded, adding a string of salty language to punctuate the point.

Simon shifted Timothy's small body from his chest to his back. The lad instinctively wrapped legs around Simon's waist, arms around his neck.

"Not so tight." He loosened the boy's grip then set his weight on the first rung of the ladder. As it swayed. Timothy's cry resounded near his ear, the wail drowning out the growing howl of the wind. After another step upward, a burst of air swooped past, swinging the rope toward the side of the ship. Simon turned his head, his cheek slamming into the hull. He hissed in pain, then used the moment of stillness to quickly climb within one rung of the deck.

Strong hands reached over and grabbed Timothy from his back. Relieved of the extra weight, Simon scrambled onto the ship's deck. Timothy launched himself into Simon's arms, knocking him backward. Some of the crew cackled laughter, but the captain offered his hand, helped Simon to his feet. Timothy attached himself again, teeth chattering, tears falling.

The captain nodded in the direction of the hold. "Best get below. You can take the boy to my chamber. We'll not lift anchor until this wind abates. By afternoon, I expect." He strode away to see that his men secured the ship.

"Just a little while," he whispered to Timothy, rubbing the boy's back. Simon attempted to roll his gait with the movement of the ship, as he'd learned on the voyage over. But a couple of

weeks on land had divested him of such skill. Still, he managed
to get them below deck and into the captain's cabin, where one
small candle sputtered in the lantern nailed to the small table.

He sat on the berth and held Timothy to his chest, praying
the storm would quickly give way to sunshine and clear sailing.

MEM STARTLED AWAKE, winced at the ache in her crooked neck.
Faint noises from the yard behind the Gray Goose alerted her to
the fact that the sun had risen. Or at least the time had passed
for it to rise. Out the window she saw only gray. Gray rain
falling from a gray sky filled with swift-moving clouds. A gray
horizon portending more precipitation.

She frowned. Little chance of making it home to check on
Simon and the crop. Or to hire the extra labor she'd intended.
Not much to be done until the weather broke. With a sigh, Mem
quietly tidied the room, the mess she'd left after her midnight
ministrations to mother and child. Arms full of soiled laundry,
she crept down the stairs, anxious to keep any squeak from
waking the girls or their new brother.

Mem barreled through the rain and into the kitchen building. An exasperated Mrs. Allen, hands on her thin hips, shook
her head at Isaac's attempts to light the fire. She sidled a glance
at Mem. "So much moisture in the air, but we'll find a flame.
Then I'll boil a kettle for those—" she nodded at the bundle
Mem carried, her voice deep and rich as the gravy in her meat
pies, "after I've got the stew simmering for the noon customers."

Mouth watering, Mem wondered when she'd last eaten as
she set the laundry in the corner and searched the table for
some simple fare to settle her stomach and give her energy for
the day ahead.

"There . . ." Mrs. Allen inclined her head toward a loaf
of bread.

"Thank you." Mem cut a thick slice, slathered it with butter from a nearby dish. In a blink, the bread disappeared. She caught a glimpse of Wilson's grin out of the corner of her eye. Before she could saw another piece of bread, a cup of tea appeared before her. She gulped it down, even in its tepidness. Her stomach yawed for more now that she'd begun to fill it.

"Likely be a slow day with all this wind and rain," Isaac said as he gathered pewter plates and utensils for the crowd that would begin arriving near midday. "I'll check in on you now and again."

Mem nodded. "Any idea if Annie will be in?"

Isaac shook his head. "I don't think it likely, between her knee and the weather. But don't worry about us down here. I'll send Wilson into the dining room if need be. You take care of my girls upstairs."

"And your boy."

Isaac's mouth stretched wide, letting her know he hadn't forgotten that he was no longer the only male Hyer in the house. Mem wiped crumbs from her fingers and her mouth before stepping away from the table.

"Send up word when you have water heated, Mrs. Allen, and I'll come down."

Mrs. Allen didn't turn, just flapped her hand in reply. Whether that meant she would call Mem or do the laundry on her own, Mem had no idea. But it didn't matter. The linens would get cleaned, as they must.

When she arrived back upstairs, Charity had awakened.

"Only a few hours and Joseph already looks different." Charity stroked the fair hair atop the boy's head as he sucked nourishment from her breast. "And handsome as his father, of that I'm already sure."

Mem smiled, her tired limbs refusing to leave the bedside chair. She loved watching Charity with a new baby. Mem reached for a clean square of cotton that would soon be soiled, folded it corner to corner, then again. Her mind strayed to the orchard, as it had so many times through the past hours. She had no choice but to trust Simon to care for her home and her harvest, even if Mr. Lott's insinuations about Simon's character hadn't been easy to discard. He was a foreigner with little to his credit. But had she extended too little confidence in him? For unlike Mr. Lott, he had seemed to accept her for herself. At least at first. When he thought her a barmaid.

She rubbed her forehead. Trust, of even those closest to her, didn't come easily. And trust of men—especially handsome ones?

She sniffed away the undeserving question as little Joseph let out a big burp before resting his head against his mother's shoulder. But Charity wasn't focused on her babe. Her attention was entirely directed toward Mem.

"What?" Mem summoned the energy to rise. She crossed the room, noticed the rain had slacked, and cracked the window to let a bit of fresh air into the close room. She angled her body, not wanting to succumb to her sister's scrutiny but not wanting to turn her back to her, either.

"At least we've kept you out of the dining room." Charity jiggled her snorting son, kissed his wrinkled forehead. "Haven't we, Joey?"

"Indeed." Mem grinned, turning her gaze out the glass, into the dimly lit day. She tried to draw in a deep breath, but the rain-washed air that wafted between sash and sill brought heaviness instead of refreshment. At least she hadn't had to clap eyes on Mr. Lott once in the past twenty-four hours. A welcome respite, to be sure. If only the thought of Graham Lott didn't also immediately call Simon to mind. His pleasing face—and even more pleasing manner. Gentleness and strength rolled into one. Like sheep's wool disguising an iron chisel.

Or a wolf.

Mem frowned.

"What about the farm? Do you need to check on things? You'll need to get the crop to market soon, or it will be worth nought."

Defensiveness rose up, blurring Mem's consideration of the man who'd come to occupy too many of her idle thoughts.

"I think I know what needs to be done." She winced at the harshness in her tone but couldn't erase it. Not after she'd already spoken. Nor did she manage to tamp it down before she spoke again. "I have to get the harvest in, but you need my help. I can't be in two places at one time."

Charity stiffened, two spots of color rising to her cheeks. For a moment, fire blazed in her eyes, and Mem braced to be consumed by the flame. But then Charity shifted Joseph from her shoulder into the crook of her arm, gazed into his face as she replied. "I didn't realize we were such a burden to you, sister. Go back to your apples. We will manage."

"Charity." Mem stepped toward the bed, but stopped short of touching her sister. "I didn't mean—"

"You did mean." Charity raised her face, her look hard and hurt. "I understand. Truly I do. Go. Check on the orchard. Manage your crop. And if you find yourself with time on your hands, we'll gladly welcome you back." One corner of her mouth tipped upward. Falsely sweet.

Even so, Mem never could resist her little sister's smile, not since the morning she'd first directed it at Mem. At less than a month old, Charity had captured seven-year-old Mem's heart as she kept watch of the baby for their mother. Mem reached for Charity's hand, her throat tight with love for the only family left to her.

"Get some rest." She took Joseph from her sister and glanced again at the window. "If the rain lets up later, I'll see if I can hire a horse and go check on the crop. But only if Annie's back to help Isaac. I'll not leave him here alone with customers to attend and a wife incapacitated."

CHAPTER 15

THROUGHOUT THE NEXT HOUR, it seemed everyone needed Mem at once. The little girls asking unending questions, followed by mind-numbing whining for Mem to pay attention to them. The new baby crying and soiling his nappy and crying again. Charity needing help with the chamber pot or asking, apologetically, for something to drink. Even Mrs. Allen, who'd come up to say the laundry water was ready. At least she'd understood the situation immediately and offered to take care of that task.

Finally everyone settled. For the moment. Mem put a hand to her head and let an exhale puff out her cheeks. She loved these people. Truly, she did. But right now she wanted to run away.

A sudden tempest of wind buffeted the building. Mem glanced at the rattling glass, waiting for the gust to abate. But it didn't. It continued on. And on. Growing in speed. In intensity. Blowing stronger. Harder. As if determined to seek a way inside. The frenzy of it set Mem's teeth on edge and whipped her charges into another outburst of neediness as one thought echoed in her head.

My apples.

She pressed her palms to her cheeks, imagining branches broken and scattered, leaves and fruit strewn across the ground. Another angry gust slammed into the building, seeming to shake it to its core.

Could wind this strong uproot trees? She shuddered at the thought of Grandfather's orchard laid out like matchsticks spilled on a table.

Mem plunked down on the edge of Charity's bed, hands wringing, numb with fear. The children's cries melded with the howl of the wind, pressing anxiety closer, stealing her breath. How would she survive the coming year without the sale of her crop?

"You'll manage." Charity pressed Mem's hand. *"We'll* manage. I promise."

Isaac rushed into the room, his usually jovial mouth pressed into a grim line. He hurried past them with barely a glance and stood at the window. Then he stiffened and dashed away.

"Isaac?" Charity's arms tightened around Joseph. "Go see." She nudged Mem toward the window.

Mem inched toward the glass, heart pounding. Another current shook the building so hard she feared the window would shatter, sending her dashing back to the bed to sweep up the girls and haul them into the parlor. Before she could settle them, Isaac burst in, set down an armload of foodstuffs then headed out again, his boots clomping on the stairs. A few minutes later, Mrs. Allen arrived with blankets and pillows, dumped them on the floor, and disappeared downstairs as well. Mem could already hear Isaac on his way up again. Perhaps she ought to take the children back to the bedchamber, out of the way.

"Let's go, girls." She snatched up Clara, told Agnes to grab Grace's hand. Charity received the children into her bed, this time speaking quietly to them, settling them as close to her as possible, her eyes begging Mem for answers.

Mem dashed to the window, anxious to evaluate the damage

of the wind and rain that had Isaac in such a panic. Though mid-morning now, the day remained as gray as dawn. Small items tumbled down the street—branches, barrels, baskets— pushed by the wind. Even a chair went past, end over end. No use brooding over her apples now. They'd all be thrown to the ground, bruised beyond selling, even for cider. Her concern shifted to Simon and Timothy. She prayed they'd taken shelter in the stone house rather than trust the clapboard barn to hold firm.

As she petitioned the Almighty to keep them safe, her gaze wandered to the end of the street, to the sea. White crests of waves rose above the wharf, crashing into the boards, leaving gaping holes on each retreat. Empty masts swayed and bobbed in the harbor, some tipping until almost horizontal. Mem wrapped her arms around her chest, a chill stealing through her that had nothing to do with the temperature of the room.

And then she noticed the debris in the street below moving differently. Swimming, not tumbling.

Dear God in heaven. Hand to her mouth, she stifled a cry as the ocean overstepped its bounds. Overwhelmed the quay. Rushed down Winchester Street. Water churning and swirling with every bellow of wind. Surging forward. A foaming river where none existed before, engulfing everything in its path. Another eruption of wind curled the sea earthward, slamming more water in to the stream already gaining ground.

"What is it, Mem? Tell me!"

Mem shook her head, feeling more than hearing Isaac's and Mrs. Allen's and now Wilson's and others' footsteps traveling up and down the stairs. They knew. They already knew.

She needed to go. To help. To—

Her mind stilled, focused on the scene beyond the window. That ship. It seemed to be … moving.

She blinked, shook her head. A long mooring, that was all. The boat tossed by this Herculean wind.

But when she looked again, the ship had grown closer, its

bow headed straight for Providence Street. Mem's hand stole from mouth to throat. She gurgled a cry, unable to tear her gaze from the unlikely armada surging toward town.

"What's—" Charity gasped just behind her. "Is that—?"

"Get away from the window." Mem practically carried Charity back to bed.

"But I—"

"But nothing. Take care of your babies. I'll get Isaac, and we'll figure out what to do." Mem pulled the bed curtains around Charity and the children before stumbling into the parlor, then down the stairs, nearly toppling Isaac on his way up.

"The water—the ships—" Mem couldn't order the words screaming in her head.

"I'll board up the window in the parlor. We'll put Charity and the children in there. I want to keep the one in the bedroom unfettered. I fear—" Isaac's expression fell in hard lines of determination. "We may be needed to help somehow."

Mem nodded, her stomach cramping with fear, her heart pounding in rhythm with her feet as she returned to Charity and the children. She helped them out of bed, then pulled the feather tick off the bed frame and dragged it into the parlor. There was barely space for it on the floor, with all the supplies Isaac, Mrs. Allen, and Wilson had managed to stash there.

Isaac arrived with boards, hammer, and nails. Mem pushed the mattress into the corner, ordering Charity down first then placing each of the children around her. Joseph squalled. Charity's bottom lip trembled. Mem leaned close, her nose almost touching her sister's. "Don't. You. Dare."

A tear slid down Charity's face, but her chin lifted.

"That's better. Now keep the girls quiet and feed that baby." Mem headed back into the bedchamber for more blankets.

THE WIND PICKED up yet again, slapping against the ship until

Simon couldn't stand without anchoring himself to something solid. If only he could climb the ladder and poke his head out of the hold, assure himself the crew wasn't worried about the squall.

"Timothy, lad." Simon doubted the boy could hear him over the screaming of the storm. He scooped his limp son from the berth. Even in sleep, his son understood to wrap his legs around Simon's waist, his arms around Simon's neck. Now if they could reach the ladder and climb to the deck without being flung down by the constant bobbing of the vessel.

Simon heaved them up one rung, then two. The tempest caught his hair and tried to tug it from its roots as he rose a little farther upward. If he could only keep his eyes open, but his lids insisted on closing. The journey was slow, but they made it. He pried his eyes into a squint and peered into the curtain of sea spray before reeling back down the ladder again and clutching his son close.

Wiping the water from his face, tasting salt on his lips, he replayed the scene he'd witnessed above--the crew lashing themselves to barrels and masts and chests. His heart threatened to beat out of his chest. If sailors were taking such precautions, he'd be a fool not to do so as well.

"Climb on my back." Simon screamed into Timothy's ear as he gave the boy a gentle push. Timothy scrambled over him, spindly arms tightening around his neck.

He forced Timothy's arms to loosen as the packet tipped sideways, farther than before. Simon gripped the ladder, Timothy shrieking in his ear, arms crushing his windpipe once more. He gasped for air while his feet found purchase. After untangling Timothy's death grip on his throat, he shifted the lad until he rested against his chest instead of his back.

Howling like a wounded beast, the storm tossed the ship side to side, tipping them farther and farther into the waves. Each time Simon was sure they would crash into the sea without returning upright.

Water rushed into the hold. Simon choked, sputtered, pressed Timothy's head against him with one hand, anchored himself to the ladder with the other.

He had to do something to secure them before the ship broke apart and flung them into the ocean's depths.

Above the wind, Simon thought he heard a snap. A mast breaking? Fear flashed through him, cold and disorienting. They were alone beneath the deck, water rising over his calves now. Even if he shouted, he doubted anyone would hear above the wind and the waves. He had to find a way out—and a rope to lash them to something floatable. Assuming he could manage any of that in the wind.

"God Almighty, help us. Help us!" He knew the words left his mouth, but he heard only another loud crack, like a gunshot. Or a lightning strike.

Or the ship breaking to pieces.

Another surge of water rushed in around them, this time accompanied by a stream of light. Gray light, but light all the same. Thankful he'd already shed his coat, Simon slogged toward the hole in the ship, Timothy clinging to him. Something bobbed past. A barrel. He tried to snag it but missed. Another report, louder this time. He had to find something to grab hold of or they would be at the mercy of the sea.

Timothy's cries turned to whimpers. Simon kept one arm cinched around his son's waist. He would not lose Timothy. If he did, he would cease struggling to save himself. For without Timothy, life would be meaningless.

The water deepened to his waist. His teeth chattered as he fought the pull of the current, determined to reach the hole in the ship's floor or side—he wasn't sure which—and hang on. His fingers closed around the jagged edge, splinters slicing into his fingers. But he didn't let go. Another white-crested wave would be gathering just behind them now. And suddenly Simon had an idea.

"Hold on, son," He shouted in Timothy's ear. "Hold on to me as tightly as you can!"

Simon fished for the lantern somewhere above his head, broke it free of its bonds, and used it to punch another hole in the battered hull, a grip for each of his hands spread wide. He pressed his son against the solid wall, chest to chest, Timothy's hands clutching Simon's sides, and prayed the weight would hold his son secure.

"Lord, have mercy!" he screamed into the tempest.

Seconds later, the monstrous swell hit his back with a thud. Simon pressed forward, praying their weight would work with the force of the water. The section of ship he held creaked, bent, then finally snapped and broke away. The makeshift raft landed hard on the water, Simon's forehead knocking against the solid boards. Had he instigated the means of their salvation or their demise?

Wind and water pushed them forward. Simon shifted, making sure Timothy could breathe, then shouted at him to hold his breath before another wave crashed over them, shooting them toward shore. Or what ought to be shore. Simon shook hair and moisture from his eyes. Tops of buildings rose before them, but there was no pier, no street, no land in sight. Only rushing water.

"Timothy?" Simon needed to know his son was safe, but even more, he needed to watch the way ahead, to be alert for the danger of debris. "Are you all right?"

Simon felt the nod, but he also felt the sobs and cold shaking of the boy's body beneath him.

He tightened his hold on the edges of the boards keeping them afloat, berating himself and his foolish pride. If they'd stayed at Mem's, they wouldn't be fighting for their lives. Instead, he'd brought them straight into the face of destruction. If only the current would slow enough to allow him to grab a stick from some other broken ship. Then he could paddle them toward safety.

An eddy caught the raft, twirled it like a top. Timothy screamed. Simon's stomach churned. He pressed his forehead into the boards and begged God to make it stop. The spinning. The screaming. If they were to die, just let them die. Nothing he could do would make a difference now. Only God could save them.

And then the raft quit revolving. Their speed slackened. Simon raised his head, took a deep breath. Buildings rose up on either side of him now, second and third story windows within reach. Could God have given them a second chance? If he could just paddle them closer. And call to someone inside to help them.

Cupping one hand, he used it to pull them toward the half-submerged buildings. Too close and their precarious craft would smash to pieces against the bricks. Not close enough and they'd sail past safety.

Then he saw it—a shadow in a window up ahead. Hope surged. He paddled harder, faster, eyes fixed on the place he'd glimpsed their rescue.

Only when he blinked and looked again, their salvation had disappeared.

CHAPTER 16

MEM PAUSED, arms full of bed coverings, and glanced out the window. The water had risen higher, reaching almost to the second floor of the building along the street. She dropped her load and hurried to peer through the glass. The ships that had been floating earlier had now been reduced to pieces littering the surging tide. Mem's gaze swept back and forth, assessing the damage, the danger. Then—

"Isaac!" Mem clawed at the sash, but the wind held the window in place. Then she ran to the parlor. "Isaac?"

He wasn't there. He must have gone down again. Without letting her eyes meet Charity's, Mem screamed down the stairs. "Isaac! Come quick!"

He bounded up two steps at a time, eyes wild. Mem grabbed his arm, pulled him into the bedroom, to the window.

"There!" Heart in her throat, she pointed to a bobbing raft, a man lying across it, holding on, his body shielding something —or someone—smaller.

"Keep your eye on them." Isaac dashed away. Mem gripped the sill and pray more fervently than ever before.

"Help us, Lord. Help us." She glanced back, noticed the

95

door to the parlor standing open. In a blink she'd crossed the room, slammed the door shut, ignored the panicked shriek from her sister as Isaac burst through the door again.

"If we can get this to them, we can pull them in," he said, dropping a coil of long, heavy rope beneath the window.

The castaways were moving closer. Mem was thankful they were still in sight, but she didn't want them to sail by. Did they even see her? She wasn't sure, though the man did seem to be paddling in her direction. She tried again to push the window up, teeth clenched, jaw tight. "I . . . can't . . ."

Then Isaac was behind her, knocking the glass from the frame, handing her the weighty cordage. The rain had almost stopped, but spray from the river in the street drenched them immediately.

Isaac wiped his face, peered out again. "The water's—"

"Isaac!" Charity's scream from the next room. "Isaac!"

He bolted, leaving Mem holding the line of twisted hemp, its roughness scraping her palms. She would save this man, even if she had to do it alone.

She leaned out the window. "Rope!" She yelled into the gale. "I have a rope."

The man's head turned in her direction, dark, wet hair obscuring his face. As he lifted one shoulder, a child, wide-eyed and pale, stared at her. Her heart jumped into her throat, and her knees buckled.

Timothy.

Oh, dear God.

And Simon.

She dropped the rope, stuck her head and shoulders through the hole in the glass. Clinging to the window sill, knuckles white, fingers cramping, she fought the storm inside her while fearing the storm without. What were they doing out there? They were supposed to be at the farm. They were supposed to be—

She shook her head. It didn't matter. They weren't there. They were here. And she had to save them.

She pulled her body back inside, wiped wet hair from her face then heaved half the length of rope into her arms and threw it toward Simon.

It barely cleared the sash, hit the water with a thud.

They couldn't get to it.

"Please, Simon. Please," Mem whispered. "Please, God. Please."

Simon stopped paddling, swiped back his hair, and met her eyes. The nakedness of his fear set her head spinning.

A chill skated down her spine. "Isaac! Help me!"

As the coil sank, the remaining rope slithered over the windowsill, into the seawater. Mem pressed her hands to her cheeks, panic's icy fingers stealing around her throat.

Simon was near enough now for her to read the pleading in his eyes. She had to get to him. But how?

Then she noticed the free end of the rope, on the floor, over the sill, into the—

She snatched up the knobby end. Held on. But she knew her strength wouldn't last, especially if Simon and Timothy were attached to the other end, trying to get to safety. She needed to secure the rope to something.

Her gaze raced around the room before landing on a table set near the bed. It couldn't go through the window. But she needed length enough to make a secure knot.

"Isaac!"

The sound of Charity's weeping mingled with the whipping wind. She couldn't think about Charity now. She had to secure the rope. She had to save Simon. Gritting her teeth, she yanked and pulled until her arms shook like warm pudding. Tears streaked down her face as her palms burned against the rough hemp. Finally—*finally*—she pulled in enough length for a knot. Fingers shaking, she wrapped the wet rope around the leg of the small table twice before tying it off and scrambling back to the window. Her skirt wet and heavy, she braced her thighs against the sill, head and chest dangling over the rush of water.

"Can you——" The wind whipped another clump of Mem's hair free from its pins, slapped it over her mouth, muffling the last of her words. She spat out the hair as Simon's hands paddled faster. If only he could reach the rope and hang on. Then she'd yell for Isaac again. And Isaac would have to come, or he'd have a man's life on his conscience.

They were closer now. Mem's heart battered her chest. If Simon missed the rope …

They needed something to slow their momentum, even just a little bit. Her gaze ran over the sparsely furnished room. Bed. Table, to which the rope had been tied. Pitcher and basin. Lamp. Broom.

Broom.

She ran to the corner and grabbed the broom. Bristles poking into her hands, she stretched long over the water, the stick extending her reach. This had to work. It had to. But even if he caught the broom's handle, could she maintain her hold?

Timothy clawed at Simon, who tried to paddle, but it was more awkward now. Took more effort. Mem leaned out farther, tottering as her heels came off the floor. Simon reached for the broom handle and missed.

Reached and missed again.

Frustration crumpled his features, but he squared his shoulders and tried once more. Mem stretched as far as she could.

His fingers grazed the tip then fell away.

In a burst of inspiration, she lowered the handle to the water, fished out the sunken rope and returned it to the surface. Then she guided it toward him with the broom handle.

Almost. There.

He stretched for it, bobbled, toppled forward.

Timothy shrieked. Their piece of wreckage capsized.

And Simon and Timothy disappeared beneath the water.

"Noooooo!" Mem lunged toward them, caught the window frame to keep herself from falling. A jagged piece of glass sliced her smallest finger. She hissed with pain, eyes fixed on the place where she'd last seen Simon and Timothy.

They couldn't be gone. They couldn't.

Then both heads broke the surface of the water, each coughing and spitting. Simon raised his arm in the air, the rope dangling from his hand.

"Hur-ry!" Bobbling up and down, each syllable burst out between gulps of air.

Both hands wrapped around the rope, Mem pulled, praying for strength she knew she didn't have.

"Don't you die on me, Simon Brennan. Don't. You. Die." She dropped to her knees, gathered her skirt in her hands to get it out of her way and to soften the burn. Then she turned from the window, slid the rope over her shoulder to give her a little more leverage, and crawled toward the bedstead. Never had a game of tug-of-war had so much at stake.

Then the weight on the end of the rope abated, throwing her forward. Her forehead smacked the bedrails. She sat back, head aching, vision blurred, as her ears registered one thump behind her. Then another. She turned, shaking head to toe, as the wind took to caterwauling again.

Or maybe the noise came from her.

Guzzling air, she scrambled to the two flopped on the floor. She cradled Timothy, lifted him into her lap. He curled against her, sputtering and coughing. On hands and knees, chest heaving, Simon raised his head, his eyes meeting hers.

Fear and gratitude swirled together in his gaze like the flotsam and jetsam outside the window. Only something else crested behind those emotions. A sentiment she never imagined she'd welcomed again.

"Miss Wilkins—" His voice softened. "Mem— You saved—" the words knotted and tangled, leaving a lump in his throat as he drank in the sight of her—face pale, eyes wide, hair dangling wet around her face. Then his gaze found his son, cradled in her arms.

He scooted closer, his shoulder brushing hers, her breath heating his face in quick gasps. Everything in him wanted to taste the salt of sea and tears mingled together on her lips, feel the strong and the soft of her.

Timothy wiggled free of her grasp and buried his face in Simon's chest. Mem looked bewildered at the sudden emptiness of her arms. Simon's hand seemed to act of its own accord, his fingers tangling in her hair, his palm resting near her ear, easing her face toward his.

The door burst open. "I'm sorry, I—"

Mem jerked back, leaving him suddenly cold. Isaac stood over them for a moment, then gathered the blankets Mem had long forgotten. After wrapping Timothy in a coverlet and pulling him from Simon's chest, Isaac carried the child from the room, the door slamming shut behind him.

Simon blinked at the quilt Isaac had dropped in front of him, still consumed with his longing for Mem.

"Let me help." She eased forward, settled the blanket around his shoulders. A trail of blood sluiced down her sleeve. As Simon gently captured her hand, her fingers curled into her palm.

He sucked in a quick breath, almost feeling her pain in himself. "You're hurt."

She shook her head, as if she hadn't remembered the injury. Slowly, she unfurled her fingers and he found the cut down the side of the smallest one. He let go of her only to tear a strip from his battered shirt, then he lifted her injured hand again and bound the wound. Her breath came in quick gasps. She started to shake.

He tied the bandage, set her hand in her lap.

"Thank you," he said, knowing the words were inadequate. "Thank you for—"

"Help me! Someone, help!" The cry carried them both to their feet.

Mem grasped the water-logged rope still dangling out the window. "Get the broom. Hurry!"

A man hugged a barrel a few feet away. Simon used the broom handle to fish the rope to the surface as Mem had done for him. Could they reach him before he sailed past?

Minutes seemed eternal, but finally the man had the rope in hand. Mem and Simon pulled him toward the window.

"I—can't—" Mem stumbled forward. Simon caught her around the waist, hauled her back toward him. The man pulled himself through the window and skidded on his stomach like a caught fish.

Mem collapsed. Then started to laugh. She put her hands to her cheeks. "I can't believe we did it! Oh, Mr.—" She sat back on her heels, suddenly somber. "Mr. Lott."

Mr. Lott?

Simon wiped water from his face, sure he'd heard wrong. Sure he'd seen wrong.

But his vision remained firm.

Graham Lott, in little more than his soggy underpants and torn cotton shirt. He must have shed his finery in an attempt to stay afloat.

Simon's lips twitched, but he corked the laughter bubbling up inside him. The man had endured a harrowing experience, as Simon well knew. He offered the man his hand.

Lott's jaw tightened, but he received the gesture with civility. Once on his feet, he tried to regain the dignity that the water had stolen from him. "Miss Wilkins. Mr. Brennan." He nodded to each in turn. "I appreciate your quick assistance. Now if you'll excuse—"

Isaac appeared, his mouth dropping open at the sight of Lott. "How did you . . .?" He scratched his head, looked to the window and back again. Then he shrugged. "Might as well come through to the parlor with the others until the water recedes. I've some ale and bread and cheese to fortify you until then."

Lott followed Isaac into the other room. Simon knew he ought to do the same. In spite of his gratitude to Mem, he needed to keep his distance. At least until he could return with a bounty of his own making, put himself on equal terms with her.

"I need to see to my son," he said, his gaze seeking something—anything—but her face.

"Of course." But she'd hesitated. Asking unspoken questions too painful to answer.

CHAPTER 17

THE SUN FELT hot on his face. He woke with a jerk, rubbed his salt-crusted eyes, and tried to think past the pounding in his head.

The gale. The makeshift raft. The rescue.

He sat upright. The world spun. He shut his eyes, opened them again slowly.

"Da?" Timothy's face appeared before him. He pulled the lad into his lap. Timothy clung to him, his tears wetting Simon's shirt. Simon rested his hand on his son's head, hair soft as a feather against his hand.

Thank you, God.

"Hush now, Timothy." Mem extracted his son from his arms and carried the child away.

Simon rubbed his temples, took a deep and cleansing breath. "How long did I sleep?"

Mem returned with a steaming bowl of something. "A couple of hours. Here. Eat."

The aroma of meat and spices curled into his nose. His stomach rumbled as he took the crockery from her, their hands brushing in the process. Her palms were red with burns from the rope, her finger still wrapped in a scrap from his shirt. She'd endured much for their rescue. His gratitude deepened.

He lifted the small bowl to his mouth and drank, aware of his hunger in a new way. Hunger for food, yes. He gulped the bowl dry. But hunger for something else, too. A hunger of the soul. A hunger he thought he'd never know again after Alannah went to heaven.

He set down the empty dish and forced himself to his feet. He swayed a moment, steadied himself with a hand to the wall. Then he noticed the lack of company in the room. The children were all there, as well as Mem and Mrs. Hyer. But the rest—Hyer, Lott, the employees of the inn who'd come up to escape the rising water—where had they gone?

"How do you feel?" Mem reached up as she spoke, as if she would smooth his hair away from his face, as his mother used to do for him as a child. But then she froze, dropped her hand, and eased away from him.

"I'm guessin' that trip down the waves wearied me more than I thought." He shook his head, blew out a long breath. "Where is ever'one?"

Mem glanced out the half-boarded up window. "The water receded as quickly as it rose. Isaac and the others went to help clean up. Mr. Lott went to assess the damage to his property."

Of course.

Simon looked down at his clothing. Soggy. Wrinkled. Ripped and battered. He couldn't walk about town looking like this. But neither could he remain idle while others worked. If he could only get—

He set his hands on his hips, frustration building like a tempest inside him. Get what? Everything they owned had been on that ship. Money. Clothing. The Bible Alannah had insisted they buy upon their marriage to record the family they would build together. Even the tools of his trade. All either at the bottom of the ocean or strewn along the street. His no longer.

He'd come to this land with little enough, and now even that was gone.

He tipped his head back, as if he could see through the roof and into the heavens. *Why, God? Why this? Why now?* His throat tightened. Then his jaw. He wouldn't give way to emotion, not in front of the women and children. But when he lowered his head, Mem's gaze almost undid him. Compassion. Strength.

And understanding.

"You'll want to help. Let me get some of Isaac's things." Mem rushed to the bedchamber.

Simon smiled shyly at Mrs. Hyer, still perched on the floor, her children around her. Only she didn't return the gesture. Instead, she slapped a hand over her mouth, her eyes wide above it. And her shoulders shook. As if she were crying.

Or laughing.

Mem reappeared, shoved clothes into his hands, and directed him to the bedroom to change. As the door shut behind him, a burst of feminine laughter sent heat rushing into his face.

WATCHING through the bedroom window as Simon strode into the litter-strewn street, Mem's insides melted and her vision blurred, tears falling without witness. Relief for children reunited with parents—both Timothy and Simon as well as Isaac, Charity and Grace, who'd dashed down the stairs determined to get something and found herself in water too deep to stand. Isaac had pulled his daughter to safety and returned her to her mother's arms while Mem had struggled alone to fish Simon and Timothy from the sea.

Drying her eyes, Mem surveyed the damage. Most of the brick buildings stood firm, though not unscathed. Remnants of ships and houses and any manner of other things cluttered the street below. Her chest ached, and her stomach clenched. If such damage had been done in town, how would her orchard have fared?

In truth, she didn't hold much hope of its survival. The winds alone likely felled the trees. And so much rain would have damaged the fruit. She shook her head, unable to fathom, unwilling to imagine.

Lost in thought, she almost didn't feel the gentle tug on her skirt. She looked down to find Timothy smiling up at her. She lifted him into her arms, let him survey the street with her.

"Where's Da?" he asked.

"Down there. He'll be back soon. Don't you worry." She pressed her lips to his temple, wishing, for a rash moment, that he were hers. But that could never be. Slowly she lowered him to the floor, encouraged him to return to her nieces before wrapping her arms across her body and letting the questions batter her mind.

Why had Simon left the farm without saying good-bye? Without even receiving his wages? Had Mr. Lott been correct after all? Had Simon been after her land?

She didn't want to believe it, but his actions seemed to put his guilt on display. Would he pursue her land more aggressively now that the gale had stolen everything else from him? Or would he do as he seemed wont to do—leave?

She bit her lip, her fingers now clutching and twisting in front of her. Even if she felt drawn to him, even if they had almost kissed, even if Charity insisted he was besotted with her —even then she couldn't take a chance. Not if it meant being loved for her possessions instead of herself. Not if it meant another broken heart.

But of all the men who'd looked her way since Papa died, she knew she could least resist this one. Something about his manner even more than his face. So she must make certain she didn't have a choice. And the only way she knew to do that was to ensure he didn't need her land.

He had a skill. A trade to ply. But he'd needed a building. A building he'd been prepared to pay for. A building Mr. Lott had rented to him then rescinded. A building now likely in disrepair.

But Graham Lott owed her. Owed Simon, too. Owed them his very life.

Mem found one of Charity's bonnets and tied it on. Then she popped into the parlor and announced she'd return in a little while. Before her sister could protest, Mem was down the stairs and out the door. Even her boots sinking into the mud didn't deter her determination. She'd make sure Simon and Timothy had the building they needed—and a few other necessary supplies as well. Then she'd have no more need to worry about her heart, for Simon Brennan would have no more need of her land.

"WHAT DO you mean you *can't*? You must." Mem stamped her foot, but the squish of the water-logged wood planks beneath her feet didn't offer the punctuation she'd hoped. "You *will*."

Mr. Lott raised one eyebrow. He no longer wore tattered bits of underclothing. And while not dressed as elegantly as normal, he was definitely attired more decently than most she'd seen on her way here. She'd had to dodge all manner of wreckage just to reach Mr. Lott's office, then again as she searched for him among his several holdings. But she'd found him. Though now she wondered what had possessed her to think she could force the man to act rightly.

He took a step closer to her, wiping a place on her cheek with his thumb. Cleaning or caressing? It didn't matter. His touch only served to deepen her disgust.

She tried to move away, but he grabbed her arm, held her near, so close his rum-laced breath felt hot on her face.

"Why do you care so much, Remembrance?" His gaze raked down the length of her, making her feel as if she ought to cover herself. "What does it matter to you if this Irishman stays or goes?"

Mem swallowed, wishing she had a simple answer to his question. She oughtn't care. But she did. And if securing the rent of this building would keep her heart free from an unfortunate entanglement, she would see it happen.

"He saved your life, Mr. Lott," she hissed. "As did I. Does that mean nothing to you?"

He let go of her arm. "My life is my own. I have no legal obligation—"

"No obligation? I beg to differ, sir. In fact, I believe should your callous disregard be understood around town, you might see the situation differently." Mem crossed her arms. "Give him back the lease on your building."

His eyes narrowed to slits before his features smoothed back to placidity. He pulled at the sleeves of his coat, brushed a bit of dirt from one shoulder. "Quite the irony, you know. You pleading on his behalf."

"And why is that?"

Mr. Lott shrugged. "Why do you think he inserted himself in our conversation at the Gray Goose that evening? He only thought to worm his way into your affections. After all, your farm is a temptation to many a man, Remembrance, though none will care for you the way I will. I'm only reiterating this because I promised your father I'd watch out for your interests. And I'm sure he understood that the best way for me to fulfill that promise was as your husband. You don't have that assurance with any other suitor. Especially not an Irishman with absolutely nothing to recommend him."

Though she hated giving credence to his words, Mem had to admit they held some truth. Not the part about Lott caring for her. She didn't believe that for a moment. The part about knowing Simon. Granted, he had been only kind and considerate thus far. But so had Solomon, in the beginning. And Mr. Lott as well.

Tears hovered close to the surface. Tears unreasonable and absurd. She had no real assurance that Simon's character would fare better than the men who'd sought her company before. So perhaps she oughtn't help him to stay. Perhaps Simon and Timothy needed to go.

"Fine, then. Provide him the means to leave. To start anew elsewhere. No amount of money ought to come amiss for saving your life."

He eyed her for a long moment before nodding. And in that nod, a dismissal.

Mem hurried back to the street, knowing the chaos of cleanup would keep her from notice. She'd disliked Graham Lott much in the past few months, but now she despised him for crushing her hopes—even if they were hopes she'd determined not to indulge.

CHAPTER 18

BY THE TIME the sun started downward, Simon felt as if he'd been plunged in a washing tub, stirred with a three-pronged dolly stick, then wrung out and hung on a line to dry. Still it had been good to put his body to work, both to forget about their harrowing ordeal and the one who saved them.

But every attempt *not* to think of her now brought her more surely to mind. He wiped his forehead with his shirtsleeve as he threaded his way back toward the Gray Goose. To Timothy.

To Mem.

He shook his head, as if that would throw her beyond his ken. He needed to think clearly, to figure out what he and Timothy would do now. He had no money for transportation. Nor to replace all the storm had stolen. He looked down at his hands, chapped and bleeding. Hands that once sculpted and sewn footwear, both delicate and sturdy. They needed to be laborer's hands now, as they had been at the orchard.

Mem's orchard. Had it escaped the damage sustained in town? He certainly hoped so. For her sake, as well as his own. After all, she'd have trouble finding help for the harvest now, with so much rebuilding to be done. Which would leave her with only his promise to help her clear her trees, if any useable fruit remained. If not, he would offer to help her clean up—without remuneration—to prove himself more honorable than Mr. Lott insinuated.

If she agreed to take him back. Even temporarily.

Simon gripped the back of his neck, relishing every physical pain that overwhelmed the ache inside. The ache that had no cure. Or rather, no cure he could allow himself to accept. For if he'd been unwilling to pursue Mem before, when he had no place to ply his craft, then he couldn't consider it now that he no longer had even the tools for such a trade.

No, he would simply have to find paid work—and for more than room and board. Cobble together an existence for himself and Timothy. Save for another run at the life he and Alannah had imagined. He wouldn't give up. He wouldn't quit. For he couldn't return with his tail between his legs and ask help from Alannah's father.

Simon stepped into the Gray Goose, the musty smell of wet wood overwhelming any scent of supper. The floor had been scraped clean of mud, except for the corners, and a few customers occupied sodden tables and chairs. At least Hyer had saved most of his foodstuffs from contamination and could limp along until he arranged new supplies.

Hyer appeared from the direction of the kitchen, face smudged with dirt and sweat. "Supper?" he said to Simon while wiping his hands on the apron tied about his waist.

Simon shook his head, started for the stairs.

Hyer stopped him with a hand to his arm. "No charge, of course. And you've a place to stay for as long as you need."

"Thank you, but I—"

"Mr. Brennan?"

Simon chest tightened as he turned, wondering what Lott wanted with him now. A thank you wouldn't come amiss—nor would the return of the sum of money Lott had kept after breaking their agreement. But Simon didn't hold any expectation of the man.

Lott cleared his throat, as if he were uncomfortable with what he had to say. Which likely he was, seeing as he owed his life to a woman and an Irishman.

"I have a proposition for you." Lott fished in his pocket, brought out a small drawstring bag, the kind used for keeping coins. "For your . . . trouble."

Simon received the weight in his open palm.

"Enough for you and the boy to find passage and a new start."

"Passage?"

"Weren't you aboard ship, headed out of town? I thought you might be anxious to continue that journey."

Simon stiffened. He'd come to America to remove himself from men who thought they had the right to rule others' lives. He'd not give in to such tyranny now. Not even if it meant scraping and scrambling for the rest of his days to make a better life for his son.

"Nay." He closed his hand around the money. His money. "I'll not be leavin'." He turned to Hyer. "We'd like to stay here, if we might, doing what work needs doin' for our keep and such."

With a grin, Hyer clapped a hand to Simon's shoulder. "Of course. I'd be most grateful for the help."

Lott sputtered, his gaze moving between the bag of money and Simon, his face mottling from pale to pink to red.

"I must see after me son." Simon turned his back on the man, climbed the stairs two at a time. New energy filled him. New strength for the Herculean task ahead. He reached the parlor and knocked at the closed door before pushing it open.

"Da!" Timothy ran to him. Simon knelt, picked up the lad. But within seconds, Timothy was wiggling free, darting back across the room. He grabbed Mem's hand, his feet dancing a jig. "He came back! Like you said!"

"Yes." Mem's eyes met Simon's over Timothy's head. Their gazes held. Taut. As if that rope that had hauled Simon and Timothy to safety pulled between them once again. Her paleness cut at his heart, reminding him that her future, too, was uncertain. Yet, God forgive him, his heart leapt at the thought. The storm might have put them on equal footing. Or close to it. Not that he desired the demise of her crop, but with a little of his money back in his pocket . . .

Well, it changed things.

"Have you any report?" he asked. "About the farm?"

She shook her head, her gaze lowering to the floor.

"Then perhaps I could escort you there tomorrow afternoon, when the roads have had a bit more time to dry."

"No, I—"

"Of course you may, Mr. Brennan." Charity stepped between them, the new baby lying peacefully in the crook of her arm. "My sister would appreciate your company. Wouldn't you, Mem?"

HEAT SINGED Mem's face as she fled down the stairs and into the bustling dining room. She froze for a moment before dashing to the kitchen and making herself available to help. She needed the activity—and the respite from Simon's presence. Especially now that Charity had made it impossible to refuse his offer to accompany her home tomorrow.

She grabbed two bowls of stew and returned to the public room, her mind working more quickly than her feet. She needn't fear going with him. After all, he would be leaving soon, taking Mr. Lott's generosity and moving on. She set food in front of two men without noting their faces, then picked up empty dishes from another table as she dodged people on her way back to the kitchen.

No, she needn't worry. She could accept his kind offer

without reservation. She was anxious to assess the damage at the farm and knew Isaac hadn't the time to take her. Nor did she have the courage to go alone. She wiped her forehead with her sleeve, picked up two full plates in the kitchen and looked to Isaac for direction.

"Back table, left corner. They'll let you know if it's wrong."

Mem headed back into the fray, politely acknowledging those asking when it was their turn to be fed. By the time she reached her destination, her head was full of questions again. She set the plates down then progressed back toward the kitchen —until a familiar face stopped her.

"Mr. Lott." She nodded politely. "I do hope our arrangement has been taken care of."

He moved toward her, his voice low and angry. "I can't be blamed for an Irishman's stubbornness."

"Stubbornness?" Mem almost groaned. What had Simon done now? Maybe she didn't want to know. Once he was no longer in sight, she wouldn't have to worry about her heart. She could return to the solitary life she'd become content with before he arrived. Before he resurrected her old dream of a family to love.

She rushed away, intent on the kitchen, not seeing the man in front of her until she rammed into his back. He turned, caught her arms.

As if her thoughts had taken form before her eyes, Simon looked down into her face, his eyes filled with concern.

"Sorry," she mumbled as she scooted past, anxious to be away from him, from the warmth his touch ignited inside her. As soon as she relinquished the dishes in the kitchen she fled, taking refuge in the stairwell. Pressing her fingers to her closed eyes, she tried to pray for wisdom. For guidance. For courage.

Tomorrow she would discover the truth about her orchard, the fate of her independence. And she would confront Simon, too. Insist on knowing the truth. For only in knowing his true motivations could she convince her heart to let him go.

CHAPTER 19

SOMETIME IN THE dark morning hours, Grace snuggled into Mem on her floor pallet, the small body brining the chilly night with warmth. Mem tried to settle back into sleep, but sleep refused to come. Instead, her mind wandered through the possibilities of the day. She imagined her stone house still standing tall and strong. But what about the fields? The orchard? The apples?

The house would have offered some shield from the worst of the wind, so maybe, just maybe, they'd find only a few leaves and small branches littering the carpet of grass beneath instead of broken limbs, felled trees, and bruised fruit strewn across the ground.

She tried to picture both images—the good and the bad. But she had no idea which one would prove true. And she suddenly understood that she couldn't change the outcome even if she knew.

She had no power over the weather—or its effect.

The truth slammed into her like the waves that had battered the wharf. In her quest for independence, she'd forgotten that she would always be dependent on God. Dependent for rain

117

and sun, yes. For seedtime and harvest. But also for strength to survive the fat years and the lean ones. She might stave off the men vying for control of her land, but she still had to surrender to the Lord. She couldn't own herself completely.

She hooked an arm around Grace's waist and pulled her closer. Mem had to be as dependent on God as this little girl was on her mother and father. Looking to Him to provide. Trusting Him to care.

As dawn brightened the room, Mem eased herself from the floor, tucking the quilt around her niece's small body, hoping the girl would sleep a bit longer. Mem dressed and made her way down to the kitchen, surprised to find Charity and the baby there, too.

"I guess you had a little visitor last night?" Charity poured coffee into two cups, handed one to Mem.

"I didn't mind." She sipped the coffee. Hot and bitter, it jolted her into greater wakefulness. "I do hate leaving you to manage alone."

"Don't worry about me. I just want *you* to have a good day." Charity's eyes twinkled. "Don't hurry back. Take all the time you need."

Mem's face steamed as hot as the coffee in her cup. "Really, Charity. He doesn't think of me that way." She hid her uncertainty with another long sip. She could tell Charity her suspicions, but she didn't want her to worry. And in spite of the awkwardness of his company, she did need to go home. To know what future awaited.

"Mem, don't assume—I mean, don't let him think you see him only as hired help. Make sure you keep other … options … open." Charity's voice had turned soft, motherly. She seemed the older sister now, with her knowledge of men and love. It flustered Mem, this switching of roles they'd played for more than a quarter of a century.

"I'll get the girls dressed for you before I leave." Mem stroked Joseph's face as it scrunched, ready to cry his need for milk. "And don't worry about me. Whatever happens, I'll be just fine."

A FEW HOURS LATER, Mem tried to focus her attention on her needle and thread as she wove it in and out of a tear in Grace's dress. In truth, exhaustion blurred her vision and made her hands clumsy. And the thought of being totally dependent on Charity and Isaac—or on a husband who wanted her land instead of her—left her fighting for breath.

Which would be worse: to lose the farm altogether or live with a man without love between them?

She didn't know. Couldn't imagine either possibility.

But she must. For the tempest winds and rogue sea had done more than break apart buildings and ships, bridges and wharfs. They had broken something inside her, too. Reminded her she had no control over the heavens and the earth. Her desire for an independent life was a phantasm after all, as Papa had warned her. Or tried to.

Charity folded another nappy and stacked it in a basket at her feet. "I love the way Timothy and the girls have taken to one another, don't you? It almost feels like he's their brother."

Mem's needle slipped, pricked her healing finger. She stuck it in her mouth, her face heating at the memory of Simon tearing his shirt, cleaning and wrapping the cut. She didn't want to talk about Timothy—or rather, Simon. She set aside the mending and rubbed her head, now beginning to pound.

"Mem? Did you hear me?" Charity was standing now, hands on her hips, looking at Mem as she did her daughters when they got into mischief.

"I heard." She rolled her shoulders, lifted her face to the breeze wafting through the glassless window in hopes that her cheeks wouldn't pink and give her feelings away, for she felt Charity's gaze boring into her even now. As much as she feared seeing the farm, she feared time alone with Simon more.

Even as she thought his name, the man stepped into the parlor, his dark hair tied back in a neat queue, looking more handsome than ever.

"Mrs. Hyer." He smiled at Charity, dimples deepening in his cheeks. A whirlpool stirred in Mem's belly. "You look well and fine this morning, ma'am. " Simon bowed toward Mem's sister without a glance in her direction, leaving Mem feeling rumpled and soiled. Beneath notice.

As if she'd desired his attention.

Which she didn't.

Except that she did.

Timothy emerged from the shadows behind him, the little girls running to embrace their playmate. In the blink of an eye, Simon's manner shifted.

"Miss Wilkins." He bowed over Mem's hand, leaving her confused at the formality. After all they'd been through yesterday, she hadn't expected this distance. But perhaps he'd already realized there wouldn't be much left of her crop and, thus, no reason to pursue their friendship. The knowledge hurt, but it also helped. "I'm ready when you are."

So he hadn't forgotten. She opened her mouth, but no sound emerged, so she nodded instead.

"Don't worry about Timothy," Charity said, her grin to Mem as full of satisfaction as a cat with a fresh kill. "He'll be just fine here with us."

MEM AND SIMON walked out of town, for nary a usable wagon could be found unemployed. Silence pulled between them as they kept pace side by side, Simon carrying a bag of food Isaac had pulled together for later in the day. The ground still squished beneath the soles of their shoes in spite of the sun that had ruled the sky as soon as the wind and sea had run their course. Wet wood and dead fish scented the air while people picked their way over pocked streets, adding to the piles of broken boards towering up every few feet. When they reached the place where the wharf once stood, they stopped, both gazing out at the placid, well-behaved ocean.

"It's hard to believe only yesterday—" Mem choked on the words, her hand stealing to her throat.

Simon nodded. "It's caused me to do some thinkin'," he said, hands in his pockets, gaze on the sea.

"Me, too." Mem looked at the ground, remembered her midnight revelation. God, who ruled the sky and the sea, He controlled the rain and the sun—the very elements her orchard needed. But elements that also contained the power to destroy. Might her feelings for Simon be of the same ilk—holding the power to foster growth or cause destruction?

Simon cupped her elbow, setting her stomach fluttering like sheets in the wind. He urged her forward, quiet falling between them once more. Town gave way to country. A pair of birds chased one another out of a nearby shrub, arching high into the clear blue sky before settling together on the high branch of an evergreen tree. There was peace out here. A peace she missed when staying at the inn. Did Simon feel it, too? She glanced at him, surprised to see his mouth turned down and his eyebrows scrunched in a V over his nose.

A small tree in the path, its roots stabbing air instead of tangling in the earth, turned her thoughts. She shivered, gripped in a sudden certainty that her orchard had been torn to bits. She would lose the crop. Maybe the entire farm. Panic stole up her throat, threatening to choke. Until she looked into the vastness of the sky and remembered that no matter what happened, she would still have God.

And Charity. And Isaac.

Simon pulled her closer to his side, as if sensing her anxiety. "Might be some downed limbs and fruit, but not everythin', I feel certain."

"I hope you're right." She offered a tight smile, wanting to catch his fervor, let it drown her disappointment and fear. But the clench of her stomach killed her hope, in spite of her effort toward faith.

"And don't worry. I'll help clean up. We'll salvage somethin'. I promise."

Mem stopped. Simon jerked backwards.

"Will you?"

Simon frowned, but didn't reply.

"Be around, I mean? You promised to stay and help before."

He winced as if she'd struck him, his gaze sliding from hers. Mem pulled her fingers from his elbow and pressed both hands against her stomach, the morning's porridge as agitated as milk in a churn.

"Why did you leave, Mr. Brennan?" Whispered words, as if she hadn't strength left to speak louder. Which made the sting of them more painful. "I thought you needed the money. But you didn't even come for your pay."

Simon clasped his hands behind his back and walked forward. Slowly. Hoping she'd follow. Believing that by keeping his eyes on the road he could manage an explanation. For he didn't trust himself to look at her. Not if it meant seeing disappointment.

Within a few steps, she'd caught up, leaving him no choice but to answer her questions.

"Aye. I needed the money. That much is true. And it was wrong of me to be leavin' as I did. I hope you'll forgive me that." He glanced over and caught her slight nod. "But after hearin' you'd be hirin' more help . . ." He let his words fall away, unsure how to continue without revealing too much of his heart.

"You didn't think I needed you anymore, was that it?" She

made it sound so simple. And close enough to the truth that he didn't balk at agreement.

He shrugged, looked away from the trust shining in her eyes. "Aye. You had help."

She pressed a hand to his forearm, as if urging him to look at her again. "I understand. But you still could've stopped by the inn. At least said good-bye. I thought—" Her lips clamped shut.

His hope rose. Did she feel the same pull toward him as he did toward her? He had a little money in his pocket now and a lot more determination to remain in Providence.

Then reality crashed in like the waves that drove them from ship to shore. Her crop might be damaged, but she still owned her land. Any attempt at a relationship would confirm Graham Lott's words. She'd think he sought her property, not her heart. No matter what he'd said to Lott, perhaps he had no course but to leave this place.

He moved away from her touch. "As I said, I'm sorry. And no matter what we find, I'll help you set things to right before Timothy and I look for somewhere to settle."

Her mouth tipped in a half-smile while tears pooled in her eyes. But she blinked them away then strode past him, setting his heart pounding at the hope that she wished he wouldn't leave.

CHAPTER 20

THE TIGHTNESS in Mem's jaws set off a pounding in her head. Where had this hope come from, this hope he wouldn't leave after all? Mr. Lott had mentioned their agreement going awry. Simon's stubbornness. Why had she assumed this meant he had chosen to stay?

Fine. So he would help, but he would leave. Again. She whirled to face him, bringing them to a halt in the middle of the road. "I know Mr. Lott offered you money to leave." She spat the words, hoping to hurt him the way he'd hurt her.

His Adam's apple bobbed in his neck, as if he'd feared this moment all along. Was she telling him what he already knew? Maybe Simon's stubbornness hadn't soured the deal. Maybe Mr. Lott had lied to her. Again.

"I thought you wanted—" Her voice broke. She cleared her throat, regained control. "What happened between the two of you?"

"I can't—" His jaw clamped shut. He shook his head.

"You can't what?" Mem jammed her fists to her hips. "The least you owe me is an explanation after I weaseled that lout into—"

"You did what?"

Mem went limp. She hadn't meant to say that. Didn't want him to know. She bit her bottom lip, wondering how to retract her statement.

His eyes narrowed. "What did you do?"

She sucked in a breath.

"Did you go to Lott?"

She confirmed with a tiny nod.

Simon huffed. "I would nev'r have asked you to go crawling to that . . . Well, never mind what he is." He grumbled the last bit before grasping her arm and charging forward.

They stalked along quietly for a few minutes, until the questions roiling inside Mem erupted without preamble.

"Why did Mr. Lott rescind his building? The truth, please."

He didn't look at her. Just kept walking, his jaw tightening and loosening in a steady rhythm.

"Why did Mr.—"

He stopped, looked her full in the face. "Because of you. Satisfied?"

Her mouth dropped open. Not the answer she anticipated. "Me? Why me?"

Simon let out a long breath, hands raking through his hair, loosening the ribbon tied at the back of his neck. "Because I interrupted your . . . conversation. In the dining room."

The truth blossomed in a moment, leaving her face hot. "Why didn't you tell me?"

He ran his hand along the line of his jaw. "I dinna want to see the regret in your eyes. Like now." He reached out, ran his thumb down the side of her face. "There's nothing to be ashamed of, Mem."

She glanced down at her clasped hands. "So Isaac sent you to the farm to help me. To make up for my being the cause of your disappointment."

"Somethin' like that." He lifted her chin, the grin on his face deepening the dimples on either end. "Now shall we go on to the farm, see where you stand?"

HE PATTED her hand where it clung to his arm, chiding himself for touching her again. Every bit of contact made it harder for him to deny the feelings inside. The feelings he'd thought would never again awaken.

He thought of Alannah, and the familiar brooding rose in his chest. She would want him and Timothy to move forward, wouldn't she? He glanced at Mem, the darkness inside pulling him deeper into despair. But her pasty complexion and eyes wide with fear brought him back to the surface.

"I can't look." She sputtered before closing her eyes, shaking her head. "What if—what if—?"

He spied her house in the distance, just over the slight rise in the road. He stopped, took both her hands in his and waited until she opened her eyes. "You don't have to face it alone."

A tear slithered down the side of her face, landing at the corner of her trembling mouth. He wanted to wipe it away, but refrained, even as his gaze caught on the edge of her lips, everything in him wanting to lower his mouth to hers.

She turned from him, and suddenly the world felt cold. Lifeless. Then he noticed her trembling. Taking her shoulders in his hands, he pulled her close, his lips near her ear, his heart battering inside his chest as relentlessly as the tempest's waves.

He hadn't expected this. Not from her. She'd been fearless in the face of floodwaters threatening his life—and Timothy's. Even Lott's. But maybe it was different for her now, her own life hanging in the balance. For he understood the orchard meant freedom for her. The same kind of freedom he'd sought by crossing an ocean.

Were they both fighting to keep their hearts as free as well? Was that wisdom—or pride? In spite of Alannah's wealth—and her father's antagonism—they'd loved each other. He couldn't deny that. And though he had often chafed at the fact that he couldn't provide the life she'd known with her father, it hadn't seemed to matter in her eyes. Could Mem possibly feel the same about her land?

He held her until she stopped shaking, unsure of the new thoughts invading his mind. Then he put some distance between them and forced her gaze to his. "You are a strong woman, Mem. You have family who loves you. And a God who will not forsake you." He clasped her hand in his, held them up for her to see. "Let's go. Together."

The spongy ground muted their steps, and the world seemed unnaturally quiet around them. Fear for her pulled tight in his chest until finally they reached the lane leading to the house. Mem tightened her hold on his hand though she kept moving. A few branches littered the way, but he knew she didn't see them. Her concern was the orchard. Her pace increased. He kept up, almost breathless as they rounded the corner of the house.

Trees lay atop one another, like matchsticks thrown from the box. Leaves mingled with grass, apples protruding from the midst. And everything—wood and greenery and fruit, on the ground or in standing trees—was covered with . . . frost.

Frost?

The closer they came to the orchard, the tighter the knot cinched in Simon's stomach. They stepped over broken branches, water-logged apples, and a ladder scattered in pieces. Walking, looking. When they reached the back row of trees, Simon let go of her hand. One tree appeared untouched, the deep V in the trunk providing a foothold. He swung himself up.

"Be careful!" Mem pressed her hands to the trunk, looking up as he climbed.

Out of her sight, he brushed a finger over the white residue on a leaf, then set his finger to his tongue.

Salt. More than just a dousing.

He made his way back to the ground where she stood

frozen, only her eyes moving across the devastation. He clasped her hand in his—shocked at its coldness—and walked toward the house. The barrels of harvested apples had broken apart, leaving her crop scattered and soggy. He let go of her hand, peeked into the cellar. Water stood near the top step. Nothing salvageable there, either.

Then she nudged him, pointed to the hole in the side of the barn. Likely all the hay had been sucked into the air and distributed over the countryside.

She covered her face with her hands while Simon stood helpless, knowing all too well the depth of her sorrow. She had nothing—nothing except the possibility of another crop, in another year. And no cash in hand for necessities until then. Perhaps even the land wouldn't be hers for long. If he offered her his heart—and his purse—would she doubt his motives? He couldn't summon the courage to find out.

Suddenly her arms dropped, and she lifted her face to the sun. "I've been neglectful of my faith in these past few months. My father would not approve. He'd say I'd put my trust in the orchard, not in the mighty hand of God. And he would be right. But God is good. He has shown me my sin and drawn me back to what I know is true." She set her hand on his arm, looked into his face. "I'll be fine. A year—or a lifetime—with Charity and Issac will do me good. And them, too, I suppose. Please, go on with your life. I can manage from here."

Her faith, her bravery, stirred his desire anew. He wouldn't leave her. Not like this. He couldn't.

Picking up her hand, he pressed his lips into her palm. She sucked in an audible breath. He winced, fearing he should apologize, but not feeling the least bit contrite.

"Will you accompany me to examine the house?" she said, gently removing her hand from his. "Now that I know the worst, there is little to fear."

He offered a gallant bow. "I am yours to command."

CHAPTER 21

THE MOLDY SMELL almost overwhelmed her when they set foot inside. She extracted her handkerchief and covered her nose as they examined the watermark left by the unruly tide. The interior had sustained little lasting damage, though it wasn't inhabitable. She shuddered, realizing how frightened she would have been to ride out the storm alone. Isolated. Forced to the upper floors with little warning or understanding.

Thank God for Joseph Gale Hyer, who'd chosen that very night to meet the world.

Simon flung open windows and doors to get air flowing about the place then together they pulled the furniture out of the house and into the sun to dry before Simon braved the stairs alone.

Mem's stomach grumbled. She wandered outside, eager to feel the sun on her face, remind herself they were no longer under threat of the wind and waves. They would need to leave soon, but the sweetness of this time with Simon beckoned her to stay. For now, he was here. With her. A memory to cherish in the long years ahead when she would have only a small corner in a crowded room. Maybe she could sell the farm before she lost it, use the money to hire a room of her own in town.

Foolishness. If her situation became that desperate, she would give the money to Isaac and Charity to help with her expenses.

Leaning against the unbowed trunk of a large pine tree in front of the house, she let her gaze roam her property and beyond. Her closest neighbor's barn lay in a heap of lumber, while the roof of their home appeared laid bare to the sky. She prayed their lives had been spared. That they would be able to put the pieces of their life back together again.

Simon joined her outside, held up a miraculously dry blanket and the bag of food they'd brought along.

She met him beneath the tall pine. "Was there damage upstairs?" Her eyes searched his, anxious to know the full extent of the truth.

"Dry and sound, but I'll have a look at the roof before we leave."

Her whole body relaxed as he spread the blanket over the ground. They ate in silence. Cheese, bread, apples. Though the apple turned sour in Mem's mouth. Two of the few greenings she'd taken to the inn day before yesterday. The only ones they'd see this year.

She cradled the apple in her hand. With everything else gone, did she have anything left to lose? She took a deep breath and let her eyes find Simon's.

"WHY DID YOU WANT TO LEAVE?" Mem's eyes searched his, as if she were trying to divine the answer. "Why *do* you want to leave?" Emotions rippled over her face, and he recognized every one. Regret. Shame. Fear. But when those faded away, there remained only ... peace.

Peace. How long had it been since he'd known it?

He thought back to his childhood, to his life with Alannah.

Love, yes. But not true peace. Only a fervent need to prove himself. To provide for her at least as well as her father could. Yes, he'd found some solace in reading Scripture on the journey across the ocean, but not enough to last once they safely reached land. It went rotten then, like apples broken open and saturated with sea salt. Only he had been the contaminator of his faith. His determination to live on his own, independent of everyone. Even God.

He knew from those long days of reading that peace came from surrender to God. But he'd imagined he could put on God like a cloak, let Him cover but not consume. Now he understood differently. He couldn't force the winds and waves to obey him, so why did he fight so hard against the One who could?

He stared out over the countryside already putting itself back together after the tumult of no small storm. If he put himself in the hands of God, asked Him to fix all that had been torn to bits, he could be restored, too. Maybe not as he imagined, but perhaps better. A stronger man, able to truly love those around him. Closing his eyes, he inhaled the moment, giving peace fertile ground to take root.

Forgive me, Lord. I never had any control, but I clung to what I thought I had. I give it up now. Surrender to Your plan, not my own.

When he opened his eyes again, Mem was watching him, the questions in her eyes as loud as if they'd left her lips.

He managed a half-smile. "I've been … remiss in my faith as well. Now was as good a time as any to correct my error." He looked down at the apple in his hand, its reddish-green skin firm and moist, inviting consumption. One of hers, he imagined, from the crop now ruined. He held it toward her, nodded for her to take it. He'd intended it as a gift of compassion, of hope, but the moment her fingers grazed his, he knew it was so much more. He tightened his hold, his hand cupping the bottom of the fruit, hers grasping from the top.

"I'm staying, Mem. In Providence." He took a deep breath as her face registered surprise. "Lott gave me the rest of my money back, but I told him I wouldn't go. Stubbornness, I suppose. Not wanting to be ruled by any man." He stopped, knowing his decision to stay had so much more behind it than simple defiance. He had to tell her. See if the hope he harbored would find its mooring.

The storm inside him quieted. "I haven't much, and I can't promise it will help you keep the farm or see your orchard flourish again. Nor can I promise I'll ever be able to provide more than a workman's wages. But my time in the floodwaters washed clean my sight, and I know I don't want to go through my days without you."

Her eyes opened wide as he leaned closer, her gaze darting to the apple held between them, then back to his face, searching his eyes, then, finally, landing on his mouth. Resting there.

"I love you, Remembrance Wilkins," he whispered.

Before he could anticipate her response, she surged forward, like waves on a gale wind, her lips finding his, her arms clinging to his neck. Suddenly he was drowning in a rush of love he hadn't expected to find—but never wanted to lose.

Author's Note

If you are like me, one of your favorite things about reading historical fiction is discovering what historical facts inspired the author's imagination to create the story. And so, dear reader, I am happy to indulge that desire.

When I happened upon the history of the Great Gale of 1815, I was fascinated by three things:

- According to a witness, "the Tempest drove the Waters through the Streets like a Sea," unmooring the ships in the harbor and sending them sailing into the town of Providence, Rhode Island, where many then broke apart and damaged buildings.
- Salt spray so permeated the area that there were reports of the rain tasting of salt, as well as salt deposits left on leaves and houses, and a salt taste permeating the fruits left on vines and trees.
- A woman watched from a second story window as a man floated past holding onto the wreckage of a ship. That man later became her husband.

As I thought about these three historical facts, Remembrance, Simon, and Timothy appeared in my head to literally weather this storm together. I loved getting to know them. I hope you have, too.

No author's note would be complete without giving thanks to those who have made this book possible:

To my team of prayer warriors: Jeff, Elizabeth, Aaron, Nathan, Debra & Kirby, Dan & Jennifer, Dawn & Billy, Mom & Dad, Robin & Bill, Leslie, Mary D., Mary L., Becky B., Becky H., Cherryl, Cheryl, Jill, Jana, and Andrea—thank you for your ongoing support and prayers. I feel them every day.

To my critique group, Life Sentence (Mary DeMuth and Leslie Wilson)—you are a constant source of encouragement and I love you both dearly.

To my editors, Deb Raney and Rachelle Rea Cobb—you have made my story and my words so much better than they were before.

To Sarah Thompson, cover artist extraordinaire—thank you for giving my dream a face.

To my children, Elizabeth, Aaron, Nathan, and Mckenna— thank you for politely asking about my work and listening patiently as I told you so more than you wanted to know.

To my sweet husband, Jeff—thank you for encouraging me to take this leap of faith. After thirty years, I love you more than I ever have before!

To Jesus, the King of my heart and my portion forever— thank you for loving a sinner such as me, and not just loving me, but changing me day-by-day to be a better reflection of You.

And my deepest thanks to you, dear reader friends, for joining me on this journey. I hope you will enjoy many more Coast-to-Coast Brides novellas!

ABOUT THE AUTHOR

Anne Mateer enjoys bringing history to life through fiction. She is the author of four WWI era novels and the Coast-to-Coast Brides novella series. Anne was a 2013 Carol Award finalist, has judged numerous writing contests, and occasionally teaches an online writing class. Anne and her husband, Jeff, have been married 30 years and are currently living an empty nest adventure in Austin, TX. They love touring historic homes, lingering in museums, and visiting their young adult children in Texas, Arkansas, and Louisiana.

To stay up-to-date on the latest book releases, sign up for Anne's newsletter here.

For more information:

www.annemateer.com

anne@annemateer.com

ALSO BY ANNE MATEER

Playing by Heart

A Home for My Heart

At Every Turn

Wings of a Dream

Contributor to:

21 Days of Joy: Stories that Celebrate Mom

Made in the USA
Columbia, SC
31 October 2017